THE STILLNESS BEFORE THE START

JENNIFER ANN SHORE

Print ISBN: 978-1-7360672-0-8

Digital ISBN: 978-1-7360672-1-5

For M, you're
forever in
my top eight

Dylan Archer wants something from me.

I don't know what it is, and I'm not exactly thrilled to find out.

I've been going to school with essentially the same makeup of classmates since second grade. Over time, we all broke off into groups and remain stuck that way. People congregate by neighborhood, sports team, and extracurricular activities.

Dylan and I fit into exactly zero of those groups together.

It's by accident I notice his interest in me—well, not me exactly, but his interest in wanting something from me.

Out of all the accidental eye catches and elbow grazes throughout the day, something is odd about the way Dylan's gaze lingers across the cafeteria.

At first, I think he's glaring at James, my best friend and his sworn enemy since fourth grade, who sits beside me. It regularly baffles me how they still have the energy to sneer at each other after all this time, but given that I have no publicly declared enemies, I can't relate.

After the third time of being distracted from my history book by *feeling* his eyes on me, I huff and slam my textbook down on the table.

"Did you do something to Dylan?" I ask James, interrupting a particularly boring—to me, not to his friends on the track team—conversation about different brands of running shoes.

He glances across the room at the same time Dylan turns back to his own tablemates. "Not that I recall," James answers dismissively. "But yesterday's practice was pretty brutal, and I did beat his mile time once, so who knows?"

"Hmm," I breathe.

In the next week, things progress as normal, but I start to become fixated on what he could possibly want.

I see him eyeing me all the time.

Walking the halls.

Sitting in the cafeteria.

Meeting Brandon, his best friend, outside the yearbook office.

Entering our English classroom like he owns it.

He kind of does, actually—his family is one of the founders of the school. Plus, his father is on the board, which is about the thousandth reminder I need that we are not in the same social circles, and I try to push the thought of him out of my brain completely.

It's difficult, though, because once I uncover a problem, I need to solve it.

Or I, at least, need to obsess over it until I find something else to direct my neuroticism toward.

"There's nothing wrong with being a planner," I remind James as we walk from Calculus to our Independent Study period in the library.

"You're right," James says. "But you're so far above being a planner that it's not even the right word to use at this point."

"How did we get on this topic?" I ask him.

"You were in the middle of lecturing me about needing to copy your Spanish homework. It's not my fault that I was so exhausted after practice yesterday that I fell asleep and forgot about it."

"It's totally your fault," I push back. "I mean, how difficult is it to look at your online calendar of classwork or, god forbid, keep track of it yourself?" I hold up my planner, which I consider to be my guidebook of existence, and trail off.

When he levels with me, I do concede his point.

"Fine, you can have it," I tell him. "But don't you need to make up that Psych test now?"

He curses under his breath as we enter the library. "Forgot," he mumbles.

Of course he did.

"You can have my Spanish during lunch," I say, and he brightens.

"You're the best, Harper Reed. You know that?"

I do know this, but I don't admit it out loud.

James heads to the counter to retrieve his makeup exam from the librarian, who is going to proctor it for him.

I mouth *good luck* before I sit down at our usual table in the back corner. As I get settled in, I notice how his face falls when he glances at the first page.

He'd definitely prefer to sit by my side distracting me or laughing at funny videos on his phone, but he has to do this exam because his mom pulled him out of school for some blood work and vitamin testing now that the track team has made it past the first few weeks of conditioning.

He's regularly embarrassed by the helicopter nature of his parents, but if I were in his shoes, I'd use it to my advantage. A few extra precious days to study? I'd be all over that. But no matter how many times I reminded him to do so, he didn't take advantage of it.

The other students continue their quiet chatter as the bell rings. I pick up murmurs of their worries about their social lives, but I tune it out to enjoy the quiet solitude of existentialism.

Just me, the endless churning of thoughts in my mind, and my planner.

I trace the soft leather cover and do my somewhat morbid but very practical mental exercise of thinking about the day I die. Every few months or so, I'll sit alone and visualize it...James and me sitting on a porch, counting the stars, each of us with a cup of tea in our hands before we fall asleep listening to the quiet summer breeze. And we never wake up.

From there, my mind works backward.

There are many steps and years needed to get to that point. Retirement, children graduating from college, long days, sleepless nights, career goals, the birth of children, a home purchase, a wedding, college, high school graduation —all leading back to me sitting in the library at this very moment.

Of course, I have plans on top of plans and contingencies for as many different scenarios as I can conjure up.

Some girls get their confidence from their looks or strength. I find it in my ability to problem-solve and micromanage my own life—I'm exhilarated by the pressure.

My sister, Audrey, gets me a planner every year for Christmas.

I don't remember exactly when she started the tradition, but this is by far the nicest one she has picked yet. It's the perfect balance between an actual calendar, a notebook, and a task list.

On the first day of school, I uncapped my brand new extra fine rollerball pen—the only kind that makes my handwriting look somewhat legible—and marked each day accordingly. Each swerve of the black ink spurred my imagination further, picturing everything I planned to experience this year.

"You only get one senior year, Harper," Audrey told me before she went back to college last August. "Try to take a break from the books and grades and live a little bit."

I bit back a retort that it would require a lobotomy for me to do that.

"I'll try," I told her, the best promise I could make in the moment.

She went back to painting my nails a bright orange color that I would remove the minute she sped away in her red Mazda. She switched subjects and had me snort-laughing within seconds as she told me the story of how she puked up jungle juice on the shoes of a frat boy president on St. Patrick's Day and got banned from their parties for life.

Audrey and I have such different personalities that if our physical features weren't so similar, I'd insist we weren't related.

When we were kids, I emulated her. I stole her make-up and clothes and followed her around whenever she'd let me. Eventually, the differences in our personalities became incredibly apparent. She morphed into the outgoing party girl who gave my parents regular coronaries, while I fell asleep most nights with my head in a book.

Just thinking about her nonsense makes me smooth down the lapel of my blazer.

Audrey had a ceremonial burning of her collection of school-issued ties, sweaters, knee socks, and the other items she haphazardly shoved onto her body as she fought me for space in our spare bathroom every morning. Getting ready has been a much calmer experience overall since she graduated high school two years ago.

Of course, most students take liberty with the dress code.

James, for example, barely attempted to make a knot with his tie this morning. It hangs loose on his chest, obscuring the unbuttoned collar.

My phone buzzes in my bag.

It's Audrey texting to ask if I can check to see if she left her favorite pink sweater in the closet when I get home, and if so, would I please mail it to her???

I promise to do so later, and she sends me a few emoji kissy faces in return.

Part of me wonders if I'm so rigid because Audrey and James are so infuriatingly lax, and I have to overcompensate.

I pull up one of her social media accounts and smile at how funny and overly posed her pictures are. It makes me miss her, like one misses the wind when it's too stifling outside, so I focus my attention on the girls gossiping a few tables over.

They're on the track team with James, and they're talking about how grueling track practice was yesterday. I already know the details of it because James complained about it for the entirety of our ride home.

The girls shift their discussion from the merits of long distance to sprinter training and ranking the hotness level of the guys on the team.

It's annoying and sexist, but I can't stop myself from listening in.

Audrey would want me to join in on their conversation, to share my funny stories and opinions on their ranking, but I can't relate to them.

I'm pretty sure the last time I ran was through the kitchen to grab a bag of chips during a commercial break. And as far as guys go, James has been the first—and pretty much the only—one on my list.

"No way," Serena laughs. "Dylan Archer over James Lawson any day."

Her argument isn't really a surprise—she and Dylan have been on and off for as long as I understood what it even meant to be somebody's girlfriend.

She's tall and sleek, the perfect combination for executing all of the jumps that make me chew on my nails in nervousness as I sit in the stands during James's track meets.

"James is the kind of boy you bring home to your

parents, ready to settle down and be seen with in public," she continues, watching him run his hands through his hair.

My best friend is blissfully unaware of the appraisal of him happening nearby. He should consider himself lucky he doesn't have to endure the callousness of girl talk.

She's right, though. James is the guy you bring home to your parents.

In fact, he's been around my parents for as long as I have. Fate, or something more kind, brought both of our parents together to move into houses next door to each other, and we were brought into this world on the same day.

Out of all the family photos hanging in our respective houses, I don't think there's one where the two of us aren't together, staring at the camera in wonder and occasionally wearing matching outfits.

He's as familiar to me as my own blood relations, and sometimes I think we're just an extension of each other.

It wasn't until our freshman year, when he had his growth spurt and made out with Lyla Gray in the hallway, that I realized I felt something deeper for him.

It's a common trope, I know, to all of a sudden fall for your best friend out of jealousy or some other emotion I didn't know how to describe, but unfortunately, I'm as cliché as they come.

But it's not like most loves I've read about. It's not some all-consuming affection; it's more like a feeling that he's a piece of me that I want to hold onto and grow with. Hence the big future plans that he's mostly oblivious to, despite how our families try to push us together.

Teenage love stories rarely have a happy ending, though, and James and me not ending up romantically involved would be devastating to everyone.

Now is absolutely not the time for us to fall into some hormone-induced relationship anyway.

Maybe after we've had some time to mature and get all the mistakes that young people are supposed to make out of our system.

More like college, junior year. A late night of studying turns into something else...

I force my eyes away from him and back on Serena's words, hoping that her objective view will hold my attention long enough for my brain to recalibrate away from this topic.

"Dylan's the kind of guy that you, well, have for everything else," Serena finishes.

Both girls erupt into quiet laughter and drop off into quieter conversation that I can't hear.

I sink back against the wooden chair and sigh.

"It's a little bit of a broad generalization, but I'll take it," a cool, bored voice says.

My head snaps up so fast, I'm surprised my neck doesn't break.

Dylan stands tall between a row of bookshelves and seems very amused at how he caught me off guard.

Finally, after a full week, I manage to drive him and his staring out of my mind, only to have him actually talk to me.

"What do you want?" I ask, wanting to cut to the chase.

That's not how Dylan plays, though.

He treats human interaction like a sport. It doesn't

matter if he's dealing with a girlfriend, a teacher, or one of the few people I think he considers friends.

There's no affection. It's all ego and manipulation.

And I can't figure out what he wants with me.

My question goes unanswered, and it's unnerving to me that he has the upper hand in whatever this is.

I feel vulnerable and defenseless, sitting at the edge of the room with all my belongings on display, so I tear my hair from the messy bun on top of my head and let the curls loose.

It's a terrible shield, but I instantly feel better.

As much as I want everything neat and organized, I've spent seventeen years unsuccessfully attempting to tame my wild hair, and for once, it's a benefit.

"Did you just try to block me out, Reed?" Dylan laughs quietly. "Using frizz as earmuffs? Hilarious."

"Are you going to tell me what you want?" I ask.

"Your help."

The two words are so light when they come off his lips that I have to make sure I heard him correctly.

Dylan Archer.

Asking someone for help.

Specifically, me.

I can't do anything other than turn back around at that, but he's already on the move.

He stalks over like a predator and takes the seat across from me. The table is a buffer, and I grip the edge like it's all I have left as a defense against him.

"I'm asking for the third and final time, Archer, what do you want?" I try my hardest to match the balance of nonchalance and venom that I know he has perfected over the years, but it comes off as an uncomfortable groan.

"Why do I get the feeling that you're not happy to see me?" Dylan asks with mock disappointment.

I look at him.

Really look at him for the first time in a long time.

He's grown into his height, filled out with long and lean muscles that are no doubt from the miles of running he does each week. His dirty blond hair is swept back off his forehead today, increasing the sharpness of his cheekbones and the severity of his brown eyes.

Dylan Archer is the picture perfect eighteen-year-old.

But there is one flaw on his porcelain skin, a small scar below his eye, and it's because of me. I, as a fourth grader, did something completely reckless and a little violent—I punched him.

From across the playground, I watched him argue with and make fun of James before hurling insults at me when I approached, and I had enough.

Audrey had just taken up tae kwon do, so part of the blame is on her for insisting on teaching me her moves in our living room. And also, to be fair, I was aiming for his nose but ended up driving the hard plastic on my finger—from my finished Ring Pop—into his cheek.

At the time, James was mad at me for fighting his battles for him, but I refused to let Dylan drag me down with him. These days, we laugh about it whenever James is particularly annoyed at him.

There's the hint of a mark, long ago healed, below his right eye. It's rounded on one end but stretches out to a line on the other, sort of like how I've seen meteors drawn.

I wonder if he sees it every time he looks in the mirror —which I imagine is quite often.

But now he is putting his ego aside, which must be difficult to do from the sheer size and weight of it, to ask me for help.

I'm equal parts cautious and curious, but the latter wins the battle in my conscious mind.

I sigh. "How can I help?"

2

"For starters, maybe you could locate a brush," Dylan says. "I mean, do you actually try to have hair that's in that...shape?"

"I see we're still in the mocking stage of our conversation," I deadpan. "Maybe we could just move on to whatever it is you need and be done with it?"

Of course, Dylan and his perfectly straight hair that's easy to style in a variety of ways finds my appearance laughable.

In the few times that we've exchanged verbal jabs, my hair and his dislike of it somehow always makes its way into the conversation.

If only he knew how many products I've tried that have failed me...

I'm annoyed, but I still try to smooth the frizz with my palm.

"It was a legitimate question," he continues, getting more confident by the second.

He leans back in his chair, and his long legs hit the fronts of my shins. I fidget until I lose the standoff, shifting my lower body so that he can sit comfortably.

"One would think a person takes a look in the mirror and sees that they have a problem that needs solving, but I'm just curious to whether you actually aim for," he pauses and gestures in a wide circle around my hair, "this."

I glance around, pleased to see that everyone is oblivious to our conversation.

Dylan Archer is a classic self-preserving narcissist, which means I don't have even a chance at breaking through his facade to hear whatever he wants me to unless it's on his terms and there aren't interruptions.

My curiosity is tangible, though. If he legitimately needs my help, it's something that the truckloads of money his family has can't buy.

Then again, I'm also fully prepared for this to be some sort of practical joke.

I open myself up to it anyway.

"Is this how you get people to do things for you?" I ask him. "Insult them?"

He bites the inside of his cheek, trying to stop a smirk.

My brain is like a reference book, not that those are used much anymore, but I appreciate their effectiveness. It's well organized, sorted alphabetically, and the one thing that I'm in complete control of at this moment.

I visualize pulling the "Dylan Archer" book off the shelf and flipping through it.

Aside from insulting James, he aggressively pursues women in his spare time. I can think of at least three direct interactions I've witnessed with Serena where he's pushing her buttons and then in the next blink, his tongue is in her mouth.

"Oh god, you do, don't you?" I realize out loud.

He shrugs. "Girls like it," he says dismissively.

I glare at him.

"Well...most girls. The ones who care about things like appearances and positive attention."

I take this insult as a deflection, stalling for whatever reason. He approached me, though, and I'm getting impatient with whatever he wants.

"Just say whatever it is you wanted to say. I've got plenty of work to do."

This statement causes him to chuckle. "I doubt it."

"Excuse me?"

"Homework is like an olympic-level sport for you. I bet you have all your assignments done through next month, if not beyond."

It's not an impossible idea, but it's not ideal. Even though I have every due date and unit mapped out in my planner, working that far ahead would be stupid. Sometimes lessons change or shift, and it's no use doubling back to do the extra work.

I did plan to use the rest of this time working on some ideas for a yearbook photo spread, though, which he is definitely intruding on.

"Are you even in this study hall?" I ask him as bitterly as I can.

I already know the answer to this question because although there are students from all four grades of this school scattered in the seats, this is the first time Dylan has graced us with his presence. Attendance is taken at the beginning of each class, even if it's just study hall, and his absence would have been noted at the beginning of the semester.

It's odd, though, that he sought me, today of all days, when James is preoccupied with taking his exam. It's almost like he planned this intentionally, which makes me even more curious as to what he wants.

"What do you want?" I repeat. This time, I am successful in being forceful.

Dylan exhales, and I watch the movement of his chest, recognizing this as a sign of finally coming to terms with something you're dreading.

He shifts, digging his elbows into his knees, before he offers me the closest thing to vulnerability I have ever seen on his face.

"English," he says simply.

"I think you speak it just fine, although a little bitter for my preferences," I tease, surprised at myself for trying to lighten the mood and make *him*, of all people, feel at ease.

It works.

"Now look who's the comedian," he mutters.

I sigh. "Do you need help with an assignment?" AP English is one of the classes we share.

"Not one," he admits. "All of them. The entire semester so far and everything up ahead."

My jaw drops open, hoping he's messing with me.

The coursework is grueling. If I'm using that word to describe it, even being as far ahead as I am, he's totally screwed.

"All of them," I repeat.

"Yep," he says as if it's the most innocent concept he has ever proposed.

Actually, it might be.

"How? Why?" I can't help but verbalize my confusion.

"I'm failing right now. I can't fail a college-level course and still expect to be admitted to the Ivy League college of my choice."

I stop myself from laughing because he seems legitimately upset. Well, as upset as someone as cold-blooded as he is could be. I'm just relying on his breathing and the lines around his eyes to figure him out.

"Your parents aren't able to just buy your admission?" I ask.

He grits his teeth. "That was the plan," he says. "I don't know if you've paid attention to anything outside of your books lately, but the FBI caught on to that arrangement for a lot of people. Now I have to get in on merit."

That last sentence seems to be particularly unpleasant for him to say.

"Sinking down to the level of the rest of us," I say. "How's that feel?"

In the few minutes of this conversation, Dylan has rubbed off on me. It's strange to actually be talking to him instead of slinging insults before stomping off. I'm gloating, and I'm surprised how good it feels.

"Are you going to help me or not?" Dylan asks, finally cutting straight to the point.

I pause to consider it.

I'm sure it comes off as malicious from his point of view, that I'm silently dragging out the inevitable, but really, I'm working out the logistics of the reading, weekly essays, and argumentative unit essays. It's a lot to handle for my own workload, let alone trying to repeat it for someone I'm not exactly on the friendliest of terms with.

It's not part of the plan, but it might be easy enough to block out chunks of time here and there to help. We could always partner up and work on it together, which might actually not be too taxing.

This isn't the first time someone has asked me for help.

Last year, I spent some time tutoring seventh graders doing a poetry unit, but in my experience, those my own age just want to pay me off and have me do everything for them. That's not going to fly now.

"I'm not doing your work for you," I tell him.

"Did I ask you to do my work for me?"

"Not exactly, but you're asking me to help you and offering up no plan or parameters, so I just assumed that was the arrangement you were interested in."

"You want money?" Dylan asks, but I can hear the disbelief in his voice.

"No," I tell him quickly.

The last thing I want is some weird monetary debt or charity handout from Dylan Archer.

His jaw ticks. "Just figure out how to get me an A in this stupid class, tell me the terms, and name your price."

"I just told you I don't want money," I remind him.

"Everyone has a price," he says, looking up from his fingertips to scowl at me. "What do you want more than anything in this world? That you've never been able to afford or otherwise have in your possession?"

Without thinking, my gaze moves forward, eyes landing on James.

Judging by how he alternates writing and chewing on the end of his pencil, he has moved to the essay portion of the test. His inky black hair is more disheveled than usual, a result of him tangling his hands in his hair in frustration.

Beside me, Dylan curses.

I turn back to him, and his expression fixes into something on the brink of erupting into chaos.

"James Lawson, of all people? Come on."

He says it like I'm one of a million girls in line, but I don't think that's the case. Even if it was, I can't imagine it's all that surprising. We're practically joined at the hip most days.

I laugh nervously, ready to brush it off, but the two girls in front of me turn around and are surprised to see Dylan and me interacting. Their gazes stay fixed on us, and they're both extremely suspicious of what we're discussing. I squirm under their scrutiny.

"Shut up, Archer," I say to him with a sweet smile plastered on my face.

He turns and follows my eye line, understanding why I'm acting like an insanely cheerful alien.

The two girls gape at him, but when he makes eye contact with Serena, something in his expression makes her turn back around and start whispering to the girl beside her.

"Your head is so far up your own ass, Reed," he says. "Or maybe it's up Lawson's? I don't know. I'm having trouble seeing it with all that hair in the way."

I glare at him.

"If you think I can be manipulated by whatever game you're playing, you're wrong," I tell him.

He considers it. "Everyone has a price. I'm just not sure what yours is yet."

I grind my teeth.

James looks up finally.

He takes in my expression and glares at how close Dylan is to me, and he turns back to his test with renewed tenacity, like he wants to finish it as soon as possible so he can come defend me from Dylan.

It's not necessarily for my sake.

I don't know if it was that moment on the playground in fourth grade that triggered the intense rivalry between them, but it's the first time I was conscious of it existing.

The tension between them increased when they both tried out for track, made it, picked the same sprinting events, and regularly finished within a half-second of each other.

I'd never admit it to James, but one of the few moments of enjoyment I got from sitting on the hard metal bleachers for hours was to watch them face off.

The Dylan across the table from me now doesn't put as much anger into their competition as James does. He seems more interested in using his domineering and manipulative nature on more important things like spending his parents' money and hooking up with girls in the parking lot.

"So?" Dylan asks, picking a non-existent piece of lint from his blazer. "Are you going to help me or what?"

"You think the world is all about using people, Dylan. It's not."

"You say 'using' like it's a bad thing."

I don't have a response for that, and I'm not necessarily

upset about it. I don't exactly know what he was trying to prove with his insults and arguments, but all it does is confirm that I want to spend as little time with him as I can in the days we have left of school.

I don't care that his cheekbones look like they were carved from marble, that his hair is perfectly styled, or that he has an extravagant life. None of those things have any effect on me directly, but they all add up to an overconfidence that grates on me. I'm not one of those people who can be bought or charmed into doing his bidding, no matter how much he thinks otherwise.

"How desperate do you think I am?" I balk.

He cocks an eyebrow. "Do you actually want me to answer that?"

Despite his attitude and the indignation inside me, I gather up my belongings and laugh. "I guess not."

Judging by his relaxed stance and smirk, he thinks he has me. "There are many things you don't understand that I can help you with, Reed."

He thinks he owns the world and everyone in it because his family has money. Even if he can't put that cash and influence he has to use, manipulation is also a well-practiced tactic, and I, for one, am not falling for it.

"Funny, coming from the person who can't even pass a class in our own native language," I say.

I clutch my planner to my chest, holding onto it as a reminder that Dylan Archer is the kind of guy who would take a wrecking ball to all of my best laid plans, with no remorse, and storm out as the bell rings.

3

I'm trying to get away from the library and to my Physics class without interruption, but a hand yanks on my elbow. I feel like a rag doll, pulled to the side with no choice in the matter, which is infuriating.

"Are you okay?" James asks. "I called your name like ten times."

I crane my neck to see the lines of concern etched into his forehead. Seeing that while breathing in the familiar scent of his family's laundry detergent makes me less angry than I was while I was being manhandled, but I'm not entirely calm.

He rubs the tops of my arms in comfort.

I should brush him off, but I know he means well, and it's nice to be cared for.

There have been plenty of rumors over the years about James and me dating because he and I are just as comfortable in public with linked arms as we are in private watching movies curled up on the couch.

It's the platonic kind of love and support that can only come to fruition as a result of seventeen years of friendship.

He attempts to stop the untruths, but it's gestures like the one he's making now, and our close proximity, that don't help to quell the spread.

I find it interesting that Dylan hasn't bought into it—or maybe he has and he was just trying to feel me out. A sinking feeling grows in my stomach at that thought.

"Damn," I say to myself through gritted teeth.

I never clarified with Dylan about my feelings for James, and now he thinks he has some deep dark secret he can hold over me. Then again, I doubt James would take anything Dylan has to say at face value since his hatred runs so deep.

Still, I feel like I should try and sidestep it with him.

As much as I don't want to, I have to come up with a plan to deal with Dylan. He's not going to let this—or what he needs from me—go easily.

"Was he bothering you?" James asks.

There's an edge to his voice, like he's hoping I'll say yes so that he'll have a reason to hate Dylan today, and it makes me pause to consider it.

Bothering me? No.

Being himself? Always.

If he had approached me and genuinely asked for help, I would have had no problem making the time for him in my schedule. But he just grated at me in a way that told me I should stay far away from him.

"Harper," James says sternly. "Are you okay?"

I nod my head, but he isn't having it.

James pulls at his mess of a tie. "I hate how he just walks around like he owns the place. Just because his family is rich and his dad is on the school board doesn't give him the right to just do whatever he wants."

"It's not a big deal," I say.

If he's this wound up about me merely being in his close proximity, I'm not going to even bother to tell him about our conversation.

"Is he even in our study hall? I've never seen him before."

"That's what I said!" I admit with exasperation.

James leans back against the wall and pulls me closer to him. I awkwardly shuffle so I can stay on my own two feet.

In the romance novel of my dreams, I would slide up, step on my tiptoes, and we'd kiss until all of our troubles ceased to exist, but in my reality, I only allow myself to reach up and brush his unruly hair off his forehead.

It falls right back down when I drop my hand, making us both laugh.

At the very least, I'm successful at making James break down his inner tension.

"Did he make you uncomfortable?" James asks.

"No," I say quickly. "But even if he did, I can handle myself. It's not like I'm totally innocent."

He laughs at that. It's one of those loud rolling ones where his eyes half-close.

I chew my bottom lip and wait for him to collect himself.

Unfortunately for me, James knows all the details of my very limited dating history.

It all pretty much starts and ends with a rushed make-out session last fall with Finn, my Homecoming date.

It's not that I wasn't interested in dating anyone up until then. I was just busy stacking my schedule with advanced classes and extracurriculars to make my college application more appealing.

Last September, I met Finn on a career day for high school seniors at one of the culinary magazine offices downtown. He and I hit it off during the lunch break over a mutual interest in a few authors and a bag of potato chips.

Frankly, I was surprised when he asked for my phone number, but I figured it was good to connect with someone who had similar interests. It didn't necessarily occur to me that he was interested in something more than building his network until he asked me out on a date.

We went out a few times before Audrey pointedly nudged me into asking him to Homecoming.

Honestly, I didn't see what the big fuss was all about with going out with someone.

Each date was a nerve-racking experience where I had to mentally flip through a list of topics that would be suitable for both of us, and I stressed the entire time over who was going to pay the check.

I much prefer to stay at home and watch reruns or eat mall food court Chinese food.

When our texts fizzled out after the dance was over, I wasn't upset about it.

Of course, James fulfills the high school jock stereotype and has been on more dates than I can count. I don't know how he manages everything while being so disorganized, but I force myself not to stress out about it.

I've been privy to the ins and outs of his relationships as well as the source of jealousy for almost all of his girlfriends. No matter how many times he tells them we're just friends, they don't buy the explanation and eventually have a meteoric breakup in his front yard.

I watch from my window and wait for him to storm over and vent to me.

"You're so cute, H," he says, lightly pulling on one of my curls.

Cute.

Cute.

Innocent.

Cute and innocent.

First, I get Dylan coercing me into doing his schoolwork, and now, I get James, my supposed best friend, patronizing me.

Neither of these things was in my planner.

The hallways start to empty, and I still have a way to walk to the science wing before the bell rings.

"See you at lunch," I tell him flatly before I'm off to Physics.

"Don't forget your Spanish homework," James calls down as I walk away.

Leave it to him to practically scream in the middle of school that he's cheating by copying my work.

I roll my eyes even though he can't see it, then I spend the remainder of the day stewing.

It doesn't help that I can feel Dylan's presence in the cafeteria as James doesn't even attempt to figure out conjugations on his own, and in my English class, the very subject he needs help with.

James texts me with a heads up that they're trail running today, so his practice is going to be a little longer than usual.

I'm usually more than fine to stay after school to study or get more yearbook work done, but today, I'm resentful that I have to wait around for him while my secondhand Honda CR-V sits in the driveway at home.

James has been carting me around since the minute he got his license, even though it was the same day I got mine —his love for driving is a sharp contrast to my excessive nervousness behind the wheel. My dad assured me I'd get more comfortable the longer I practiced, but it hasn't happened yet.

By the time I head to the yearbook office after school, my annoyance has turned into an anger that won't ease up.

I snap at everyone who asks me questions about copy and layouts enough times that people start to leave me alone.

Kyle Gray, a lanky brunette who I normally consider a friend, stage whispers to his twin sister, Lyla, about what a total nightmare I'm being.

It's not my fault that his pages on the football team championship were subpar. Honestly, I could have designed them better myself with my eyes closed.

Brandon, Dylan's best friend, watches me angrily type on my ancient laptop, but he's smart enough to keep his distance.

I thought it was odd that Brandon approached me a few weeks ago to ask if there were any vacancies on staff, but now, I'm seeing his presence in the vein of Dylan's manipulation.

Dylan has now managed to infiltrate my Independent Study, lunch hour, favorite subject, and after school crowning achievement.

I try to focus on my duties as editor-in-chief, but I'm just wasting time and energy.

Eventually, I throw in the towel, knowing that harping on the staff when they're already working hard isn't going to be productive.

"I'm leaving early today," I tell no one in particular.

"Thank god," Kyle breathes.

I don't acknowledge it.

As I stroll through the school hallways, I appreciate the quiet and am grateful for the time to decompress alone.

The school practically buzzes with excitement during the day, then the second the last bell of the day rings, it's a ghost town, except for those of us with extracurriculars and nowhere else to go.

I used to dream of what it would be like to be a senior. I always imagined myself as some sort of badass, strolling through the halls in a pair of leather pants or high heels or something.

I'm the furthest thing from it, and the realization makes me frown.

My mind is too off-kilter for self-criticism right now, so I try to shake that thought off as I step outside.

The March air is cold, but I'm warm enough walking in the sunshine.

The unpredictability of the weather is infuriating for a planner like me. In our Pennsylvania town, we go from sixty-five degrees one day to a foot of snow the next.

I walk along the sidewalk, leaving my jacket unbuttoned

to maximize the rays on my skin, until I reach the entrance of the stadium. A few students and parents take advantage of the vacant track, but it's mostly empty.

I drag my fingers along the stone wall until I find a place to sit in a patch of grass on the opposite side of the locker room. I usually wait for James by his car or in the yearbook room, so he won't be expecting me out here.

After shooting him a quick text about my location that he'll get when he returns, I aimlessly scroll social media.

Before I can talk myself out of it, I seek out Dylan's profile.

I'm not surprised to see it's completely blank. He doesn't have any posts, but he's following a few people from the team. Brandon is the only person who regularly tags him in photos, and Dylan doesn't appear to be a willing participant in them.

Still, he has nearly one thousand followers—that many people want to follow him even though he doesn't have any pictures or videos.

I flip over to my feed and my two hundred followers.

Like his, my account is nearly empty, but the difference between our lack of posts is that he comes off as mysterious and I'm just boring.

Dylan Archer is the antihero.

I've read more than enough books to recognize the signs, to be allured by his darkness and hope for a redemption arc, but I know that won't happen. He'll use me to help him get out of this town, just like we're all trying to do, and I'll never hear from him again.

Still, part of me feels bad for him.

The anger dissipates as I think about the internal

struggle Dylan had to go through to be able to ask for help. As prickly as he is, I can't imagine it was easy for him to swallow his pride and approach me.

Guilt, I learn, is an antidote for rage.

The tips of my fingers start to freeze as he appears at the side entrance of the track.

He's the first one to arrive back from whatever torture of a trail run their coaches put them through today.

"Dylan," I call out to get his attention.

His chest heaves as he approaches me.

Hands on his hips, pale skin blotchy and dotted with perspiration—it's fascinating to see him imperfect.

I blink and realize I've already decided that I'm going to do whatever it takes to get him an A in class even though he probably doesn't deserve it.

This is going to cause some major adjustments to my planning.

"Reed," he says as he expels a huge breath from his lungs.

"Stop calling me by my last name," I sputter somewhat coherently. "We're not on a hockey team or in some sort of boys' club together. 'Harper' does have two syllables, but I think you're capable of saying it."

He sighs. "If you've called me over here just to berate me on semantics, I'm going to leave."

"Is that the attitude you want to give to someone who's willing to help you?" I ask him, shielding my eyes from the sun.

A flicker of something, surprise maybe, surfaces on his expression. Before I can take it in fully, he's back to shrouding himself with indifference.

I gesture for him to sit beside me so I don't have to extend my neck or stare into the light to continue this conversation.

He hesitates before he lowers himself beside me on the grass.

"Don't let this go to your head. I'm not doing this because of your supposed overt charms. If anything, your exceptional personality has me second-guessing this every second." I pause for emphasis. "Let's get your grade back up and then we can both move on and go back to pretending like the other person doesn't exist."

I force myself not to watch the rise and fall of his chest as he considers my words, but it's hard not to. I see every movement through his skin-tight running shirt, and the inhales and exhales are the only sound in my ears as I wait for him to respond.

"But just to clarify, I don't need your help with my dating life," I add.

He cocks an eyebrow. "Your non-existent one, you mean."

I resist the urge to snap at him.

I'm trying to be the definition of civility in every single one of our conversations. It's the only upper hand I can have.

"Just please keep our conversation this morning between us," I say quietly, looking at my fingers as I speak. "It will ruin pretty much everything for me."

He props himself up on his elbows. "So dramatic, Reed," he teases. "Who do you think I am? Some sort of idiot, running around spreading nonsense?"

I shrug, watching some of the other runners, including

James, return to the locker room. I'm glad we're tucked away enough that they seem completely oblivious to the close proximity and false intimacy of the closeness between Dylan and me.

This is an academic arrangement, not a friendship or anything remotely close to it.

"Fine," Dylan finally says. "It's a deal. An A in English, and I'll keep my mouth shut."

Dylan got me to crack in under six hours after just one conversation with him. It seems pathetic, but it might actually be a record for his persuasive efforts.

"And maybe we could keep our distance at school?" I suggest.

"Why? Do you think people will think we're together?" He chuckles. "Me and *you*. And that *hair*. That won't be a problem."

"Just because I've agreed to help you doesn't mean you can insult me whenever you like. Keep it up, and I'll give you another black eye." I try my best to sound serious and threatening, but it's comical considering he's a good eight inches taller than me.

He scoffs. "I'd hardly call it a black eye."

It was technically cut below a purple eye that puffed up for about a week until it faded into a disgusting yellow-green color.

"What would you call it?" I asked him. "A lucky shot?"

The corner of his mouth ticks. "Undeveloped reflexes, which I can assure you is no longer the case."

He's definitely insinuating something.

I blush instantly, feeling the splotchy red forming on my

neck and cheeks, which is pathetic considering he's just saying it to make me uncomfortable.

Maybe James was right. I am innocent. And *cute*.

I shake away that thought and the emotion with it.

"Whatever it was, you deserved it," I insist.

"I can't entirely agree with that."

He's been quick-witted and callous for as long as I can remember. I assume it's a genetic trait, passed down from his parents and their generational wealth.

It's not lost on me that the one born with every opportunity has to stoop down to ask the partial scholarship kid for help with something so important in his life.

He stands and stretches his arms overhead, and I divert my eyes from the exposed skin of his stomach.

I play with the fraying strap of my bag, but I stop once I realize he is watching the movement with a frown.

He's going to have to get used to the secondhand, non-designer things around me.

"So, I'll text you later with a study schedule," I tell him.

I'm lame enough to have already entered everyone's numbers in my phone from the school directory. This is the first time, outside of yearbook-related activities, it has actually come in handy.

My mind already starts to plot the best way to make up the past units and intersperse them with the current workload he has likely abandoned. But I suppose I'll have to gauge how fast of a reader he is before I finalize everything.

"You're actually looking forward to extra work, aren't you?" Dylan laughs. "I can practically see your brain getting excited."

I wave him off toward the locker room, as if I'm some sort of princess and he's a fly buzzing around me.

But he doesn't move.

"Did you want to fit one final insult in before you foam roll?" I ask.

He rolls his eyes. "Do you need a ride home?"

"Oh, no," I say, unable to hide my surprise. "Thank you, though."

This doesn't match up with what I know about his character. Polite and concerned for my well-being aren't exactly traits I associate with Dylan Archer.

Manipulative and smug? Yes. Selfless? No way.

He eyes me like he doesn't believe me. "If you're planning to hitchhike, I can assure you that no one is going to bother to slow down for that hair."

I involuntarily snort. "But you would?"

"Against my better judgment."

And there it is—the insult.

He can't even do something nice without having a sharp edge.

But I don't think he's going to leave until I tell him the truth, so I do. "James is driving me home."

"Does he do this every day?" Dylan asks.

"Yep."

In exchange, I buy him coffee and donuts every Friday and don't complain about whatever terrible music he forces me to listen to. I don't know how he can stand listening to heavy metal early in the morning sometimes, but I've chosen to look past it.

Of course, I keep this information to myself.

"Do you not have a car?"

"Of course I have a car," I tell him. "I know that you're, like, ungodly wealthy, but us scholarship kids are doing just fine."

"So, you're just voluntarily waiting around all pathetically for James to cart you home?"

I don't bother answering that sneer.

"That's...not good," Dylan sighs.

"What could possibly be wrong with carpooling? It's better for the environment. Convenient. And I can read on the ride to school."

Dylan crosses his arms over his chest, a nonchalant move on anyone but him. "You need to start driving yourself."

"But I hate driving," I admit. "James doesn't mind, honestly."

"It's not sexy to be a burden."

"I hardly think I'm a—"

"Let me give you some free advice, Reed, since you're doing me a favor and all," he says, facing me as he walks backward over to the locker room. "Don't sit out in the cold, waiting for someone to validate your existence. Get some of your own goddamn independence."

I frown.

I'm many things, but I like to think I'm some degree of self-reliant. Hell, I've taken the planning of my entire life in stride.

Independence might as well be my middle name. Or maybe fortitude.

When he sees me not taking his demand seriously, he adds, "Girls think that guys have this innate need to care for them, but we're all selfish bastards. It might be better for the environment, but it's bad for you. Trust me on this."

For some reason, I do.

It might be because I don't have any other option.

"Fine," I huff. "I'll drive myself to school tomorrow if you're so concerned for my existence and self-worth."

"A 'thank you,' works just as well, you know."

I laugh.

Somehow I got roped into doing a favor through insults. I guess he's right—his approach really does work.

Well, on teenage girls at least. But, unfortunately for him, I don't think he can go crying to his school board father. In fact, I bet he'd be furious if he knew his son was failing.

"Archer," I say, purposefully using his last name to catch his attention once more. "Be prepared to grovel tomorrow."

He quirks an eyebrow, waiting for me to continue.

"You're going to have to use your *skills* to get Miss Delway to let you catch up on everything from this semester so far," I explain. "She doesn't really like to give second chances."

He rolls his eyes. "That won't be a problem."

That won't, but I have a feeling everything else will be.

4

James is quiet on the ride home.

He's tired and distracted enough to let me pick the music, which is rare.

My French Indie playlist is the perfect soundtrack to zone out to as he drives. Even though I have no idea what they're saying, I've been obsessed with it lately. It's a one-eighty from the stuff he insists on blaring through his speakers every morning.

And starting tomorrow morning, I'll be able to listen to whatever I want, setting the soundtrack for my day on my own terms.

"Hey, James?"

"Hmm?" he hums in the back of this throat.

"I'm going to start driving myself to school from now on," I say quickly, ripping it off like a bandage.

He blinks but doesn't say anything right away.

One benefit of being in the passenger's seat is that I get the opportunity to ogle his side profile whenever I want, but he doesn't get that luxury. Once we idle at a red light, he studies me.

"Is this about the track and field spread in the year-book?" James asks. "Because it was all Lyla's idea, not mine."

I pause. "What about it?" I ask slowly.

"Nothing," he says too innocently for me to believe that he's telling the truth.

"James."

"It's really nothing. Just an idea she had, and I thought it sounded like a good one."

I glare at him.

"She's going to talk to you about it tomorrow," he explains. "I don't want to butcher her vision by trying to explain it to you now."

"Her vision?" I balk. "Let me guess. She wants to do a big story on you with a full photoshoot where you're indoors but somehow replicating your running moves in a studio?"

He looks sheepish when I put it plainly. "Well, yeah, kind of."

She had the same idea for whatever wrestler she was seeing in December. I hated it then, and it's not going to fly now. It'll totally disrupt the theme, and I don't need whatever she considers *cool* to be in the pages of something I've had vision boards for since eighth grade.

"And this definitely doesn't have anything to do with the fact that she's looking for an excuse to pick up where you guys left off freshman year? Or last summer behind Dairy Queen between your shifts? Because as my best friend, you certainly wouldn't be happy to use this as an excuse to get in her pants?"

"Definitely not," he quips.

James is the first to admit that he has a blind spot for my feelings sometimes, and this has been a hell of a day for it.

"No, James," I say bitterly, "this has nothing to do with why I'm going to drive myself to school from now on."

I turn up the music and force my stare out the window.

He doesn't fight me on the issue, and I'm both relieved and disappointed by it.

Maybe Dylan was right; I do need some independence, which is a painful realization on so many levels.

The rest of the ride home drags on, and by the time James pulls in his driveway, I'm fidgeting to get out.

"You'll still come to my meet next week, right?" James calls to me as I walk toward the front door.

My back is to him, so he doesn't see the pinched expression on my face.

"Of course," I say evenly.

I've never missed one. I still went even when we were in a huge fight for a week of sophomore year over some stupid Chemistry presentation we partnered up on.

I suppose that's part of life with someone—fighting, making up, moving on, but keeping it a part of the shared history between us. I already know that part of life with James means we're going to have one thousand more moments like this, but it's worth it.

At least, I hope it is.

When I glance over my shoulder, James smiles at me.

It's one of his heart-stopping, half-shy smiles that morphs into a grin that goes all the way up to his eyes.

Usually, it makes me weak at the knees, but something about it feels hollow today.

I tear my eyes away and head inside.

Thankfully, the next few hours are uneventful. I do homework until it's time for spaghetti dinner with my parents.

We all fill each other in on what has happened in the past twenty-four hours since we last sat down together and laugh collectively at the texts Audrey sends us during the day.

As far as parents go, mine are good ones—they're involved in my life but not overly so.

It's the exact opposite of James's parents. His mom makes him share the location of his phone with her so he can be accessible at all times. Once he and I made a wrong turn while trying to find a new coffee shop, and she called us within five minutes to ask why we weren't on the way home.

James is an only child and their one chance at doing it right. My parents got all of their overprotective tendencies out on Audrey, who rebelled enough for the both of us.

Sometimes I think my parents are genuinely surprised that I don't go out and find trouble for myself.

Last fall during their anniversary weekend trip, they made a joke about how it was a rite of passage to throw a rager when you're home alone. James and I split a wine cooler, ordered pizza, and watched old episodes of *The Office*.

I'm pretty sure the house was cleaner when they arrived than when they left.

My dad swirls the pasta on his fork, trying and failing to set himself up for a manageable bite. "How's your essay coming along, H?"

"Same as yesterday," I tell him.

I aggressively smush the soft piece of garlic bread into the red sauce in my bowl, taking out my frustration on delicious carbohydrates.

The Pittsburgh Press, a small local publishing company, is hosting a writing contest for all high school seniors in the area.

Entering it alone is a great opportunity to get my name and writing in front of professional writers and editors, but winning comes with the option to intern with them next summer.

My reputation as an overachiever is falling short on this one.

I have grandiose dreams about being able to sit down and write the most amazing, witty, but not condescending, essay that will guarantee a win, but when I actually try to make it happen, I overthink it to the point of stifling myself.

I know exactly what I want to say, but it gets lost in the process. When I try to write it down, it's too cheesy or melodramatic, and I end up tossing it aside.

I'm running out of time, though.

The deadline is approaching quickly—of course, it's already blocked out on my planner. If I don't come up with something soon to write about, I'm going to miss out on a huge opportunity.

I wish the prompt was something easier that I could write after some research or inspiration, but it's a personal essay, sharing the story of your life.

I'm supposed to sum everything up in under one thousand words, but the only problem is that I can barely get two paragraphs in before I've run out of material. It's exceedingly frustrating for someone who is accustomed to turning in papers that are twice the requested word length in school.

I live in my own head, not through action. I'm starting to realize that is definitely going to be a problem.

"It'll come together soon," my mother attempts to reassure me.

I give up on the rest of my dinner, brushing the crumbs from my hand back into the bowl.

My dad jumps in. "And it's totally fine if not. Lord knows you put enough pressure on yourself, Miss Valedictorian. You're allowed to give yourself a break."

"Yeah," I say, not totally committing to it.

"There will be plenty of other contests and internships."

I hope so, but this would be huge for me, being able to get experience here in Pittsburgh over the summer, rent-free. This city isn't exactly a hotbed for publishing and writing jobs, so securing this one now would be one less thing to worry about in the future.

I have an innate ability to lose sleep over something that's months or even years away from happening. I get ahead of myself, I know this. My obsession with organization and planning has been good to me so far, but I curse it during the nights I toss and turn.

We finish up and clean up, then they send me up to my room with dessert to do work and not write my essay.

I slurp down the half-melted ice cream as I dig through Audrey's closet. It's somehow still packed even though she drove back to school over Christmas with a car filled to the brim. I find the sweater she texted me about earlier and promise I'll have mom include it in her next care package.

For the remainder of my sugar high, I'm in planning mode.

I rifle through all the papers in my filing system until I find the AP English syllabus. I spend two hours mapping out a plan to get Dylan caught up, if Miss Delway will even let him do so.

By the time I brush my teeth, my brain is tired enough to rest.

I sleep hard, and I actually feel good as I get ready the next morning.

As much as Audrey cursed the uniform, I feel like some part of her had to appreciate the simplicity of it. Of course, she was one of those people who skirted the rules with patterned black tights instead of solid ones, and I'm a rule follower to a fault.

I stare at my reflection a little longer this morning.

But what if I wasn't so rigid? What if I just let everything go? Let Lyla do her wild idea? Skipped a few reading assignments? Was late for a class?

I shiver at that thought and laugh at my reflection.

That's not me at all, and I don't mind it. I'm not out for some overhaul of my personality in the last one hundred days of school.

There's absolutely nothing wrong with being a smart, forward-thinking woman who knows what she wants.

And I do want to be a little rebellious today. After all, I'm going to *drive* myself somewhere, which is a big enough deal on its own.

I just want to have a little secret, just for me.

I dig through Audrey's jewelry box and find a pair of lotus flower earrings from her boho phase. They're silver and simple, but they dangle off my earlobes.

The school dress code clearly states that simple hoop earrings smaller than one centimeter or plain studs are the only suitable ear jewelry. They explicitly prohibit a number of other piercings, and I didn't even know there were that many options until I read it listed out in the school rules.

Why the school board feels like they have to police these kinds of things, I'll never know.

I put them in and shake out my hair. It's so unruly and voluminous that no one could find my earlobes if they tried, but I know that they're there.

And I like how that makes me feel.

"You're driving?" My dad can't hide the amusement in his voice when I take my car keys off the hook. "Is there a layer of dust on those keys?"

They know better than anyone how reluctant I am to drive. I'm a nervous driver, always trying to look thirty places at once and convinced that I'm going to get in an accident.

My mom hands me an apple and granola bar for the road. "Is James not feeling well?"

"No," I say casually, but it's clear they're waiting for me

to elaborate, so I scramble for a lie. "His practices have been going later, and I don't want to sit around at school."

They seem to buy that, so I head out.

The most challenging part of my morning is finding a close parking spot in the lot.

Calculus, Independent Study, and Physics are inconsequential, and the day feels like any other until I step in Miss Delway's classroom for AP English.

We don't have assigned seats for any of our classes at school. Some people shuffle around, but I sit front and center at every opportunity. It's easier for me to focus on the lectures without the temptation to sit back and mess around on my phone under my desk.

I catch Dylan's gaze before I sit.

His expression is smug and maybe a little challenging.

He tilts his head to the left, a silent request to fill the vacant seat beside him. Part of me wants to defy him just to show that he doesn't have any power over me. But a deal's a deal, and I can't very well micromanage his education by sitting across the room.

"I'm guessing Miss Delway gave you the green light?" I ask quietly.

It's an odd move for me to talk to Dylan calmly, let alone sit beside him, so I'm not surprised at Serena's gawking as I settle in.

He shrugs. "Something like that," he says.

I don't like how it's mostly a non-answer.

I assume his indifference isn't because of the prying eyes around us but because he knew outright it wouldn't be an issue.

Must be nice to have the expectation that the world is yours.

"I wish my father was on the school board," I say. "Built in intimidation to get what you want."

Dylan doesn't seek out trouble, but having Andrew Archer and his power in your back pocket is a trump card. He can do things like skip class and stalk me in Independent Study without so much as a warning for detention.

"I don't need my father to do my work for me." There's a bite to his retort that makes me want to retreat.

I've hit a nerve.

Interesting.

"You just need me then?" I tease.

He rolls his eyes.

Miss Delway steps up to the podium at the front of the class, commanding our attention as the bell rings.

She doesn't notice or acknowledge my change in location. If anything, she's probably grateful I'm not in her line of sight.

Despite how much I love English and writing, I'm actually probably her least favorite student.

Miss Delway is an accomplished non-fiction writer, with a bestseller and a few co-published books to her name. She indulged my questions and interests at first, but I think I overwhelmed her with my excitement.

Over time, my emails went unreturned, and she began to make excuses for why she could no longer recommend and discuss books after class unless they were explicitly related to what we were working on.

I bet she'd indulge Dylan's questions.

"We're starting our unit on dystopian literature today,"

Miss Delway announces, pulling up her presentation. "Who can tell me the difference between dystopian and utopian literature?"

My hand shoots up. I'm ready to answer with their definitions, how they differ, and a few examples of each.

She doesn't call on me, even when Serena gives a short, unimaginative answer.

Miss Delway is satisfied, though.

She begins her long and somewhat dry lecture, spending thirty minutes walking us through her presentation. I take avid notes on common tropes and themes, which will definitely be helpful for some of the upcoming assignments.

I recognize a number of the authors and understand the influences they had on each other.

After I jot down a list of books to check out during Independent Study tomorrow, I notice that Dylan's lost in thought.

One would think that being motionless meant he was absorbing every word of the lecture, but one glance tells me he hasn't heard a word Miss Delway has said. My instinct is to snap my fingers in front of his face, but that would bring more attention to me than anything else.

His calmness makes me hyper-aware of my restlessness. I'm constantly readjusting how I sit, twirling a pen in my hand, and smoothing down my hair, but he's just...there.

Breathing and existing and actively not doing anything.

That's going to be a problem.

"What book are you selecting?" I ask Dylan as Miss Delway sits back at her desk.

"Whatever one you pick for us."

For someone who likes to have the upper hand, it's a little surprising and infuriating that he cares so little about this.

"I'm not doing the assignments for you," I remind him.

The last thing I need is another one of those situations where I'm stuck doing the work of four people. Without fail, it's what happens for every group assignment.

"I know," he says in a bored tone. "I don't have a preference, and I'd rather just to do whatever you're doing if we're going to do the assignments at the same time."

"Fair enough," I admit. "I think I want *Brave New World*. I read it a few years ago and loved it. There's plenty to work with for the assignments and unit paper she wants us to do."

He yawns. "Fine with me."

"And Huxley had a remarkable influence on almost every single dystopian novel that was published after it."

I'm getting excited just thinking about it. It's so cool to see trends and patterns in books and to think about how one book can have a legacy that carries through an entire genre and over multiple generations.

Dylan does not share my enthusiasm.

"Why are you even bothering going to college?" I ask because I can't help it. "Doesn't your dad have a job waiting for you the second you graduate?"

He doesn't realize how privileged he is to be at this school and queued up for a spot at the Ivy League school of his choice.

And I'm enabling it.

"Maybe I have my own plans," he answers. "Or maybe I just want to get the hell away from this place."

Both of those seem believable enough. "Are you going to tell me which school you're applying to?"

"Does it matter? They're all cold in the winter."

Of course that's his answer.

He doesn't have to worry about which school is going to offer him the most scholarship money, if there are cheaper off-campus rooms to rent, or what his parents think about him moving so far away.

"The campuses are so different, as well as the specialties in academia," I say as neutrally as I can. "You really don't care about where you're going to spend four years of your life?"

"Well, since you're so well versed, why don't you tell me your top pick?"

I think he's going to brush me off once the bell rings, but we fall in stride beside each other and walk toward the cafeteria.

"James wants Cornell and—"

"Did I ask where he is going?" Dylan sighs.

People watch us walk together.

It's hard to miss it because the normally crowded hallway parts like the Red Sea to let us through.

We're an unusual duo. The bookworm and the bad boy.

It's like a really weird fairytale, but instead of falling in love, he's using me and keeping my secret, and I'm okay with it.

Except for the fact that I don't like to be the center of attention.

I run my hands through my hair, pulling it down to frame and hide my face when I dip my head down.

Dylan doesn't notice the stares or my discomfort; he just side-eyes me and waits for my answer.

I really have nothing to lose by telling him the truth, so I decide to do so, regardless of how much it will irritate him.

Actually, that might be a bonus.

"Our families are rooting for us to go together," I explain. "We live next door to each other. We have for my entire life. I mean, we were born on the same day in rooms on the same floor of the same hospital. Our parents are best friends, and James is mine. It just kind of works out to go along with it."

Dylan considers my explanation.

As if he, of all people, would understand what it's like to make promises and have loyalty toward other people. "But you don't want to go there?"

"Cornell's a great school. And it's kind of selfish because I'm so lucky to be able to go to college at all. Well, pending financial aid. But the thought of spending four years in the middle of nowhere in New York State..." I trail off.

"Sounds boring as hell," Dylan finishes my thought when we enter the cafeteria.

"It's a really beautiful campus, though. The architecture is interesting at least."

He wrinkles his nose. "If that's your selling point, I think I'll cross that one off the list."

We're in line with our trays in our hands, and I can feel his stare, waiting for me to tell him my choice.

It's an easy word to say, but it's an admission I haven't made to anyone.

Not even my parents.

Certainly not James.

They all know I've applied to multiple schools and for numerous scholarships, but I told them I wanted to wait until I had all the letters to officially make the decision. Still, they've all dropped plenty of hints that it wouldn't be so bad to be at school together.

"Columbia," I say quietly.

"Colombia? Do you even speak Spanish?"

I'm about to correct him, but the upturned corner of his mouth reveals that he's messing with me.

"Relax, Reed," he says, sliding one of the rice and chicken dishes onto his tray. "What's another little secret between classmates?"

I swallow. "Well, that's my dream. Life in New York City."

"Some people say it's overrated," he says.

"Overrated? It's the cultural epicenter of the U.S. Restaurants, museums, and oh my gosh, the library." I smile. "I want to spend days of my life in that building."

"What's stopping you?"

There are a lot of reasons, but I give him the one that's the easiest to explain. "On our thirteenth birthday, James and I made a pact that we'd go to college together."

Dylan waits for me as I load my plate up on items from the salad bar.

I'm practically shaking at the novelty of this, talking to him while others gawk, but honestly, it's not as bad as I thought it would be. I'm just trying to ignore them as well as he does.

I thank Loretta, the head of culinary, while Dylan half-nods in her direction.

"So, you're following someone to a school you don't even want to go to when you have dreams to go elsewhere," he finally says. "That's stupid."

"It's not stupid. It's called 'friendship.' Loyalty means something to some people, you know."

"This is not loyalty. This is basing your life off of a decision you made as you became a teenager, which is, as I said, stupid."

I open my mouth to cut him off, but he keeps going.

"What you did when you were thirteen doesn't count," he insists. "Want to know what I was doing when I was thirteen?"

"Manipulating fifteen-year-olds into letting you feel them up?"

At this, he laughs out loud, calling even more attention to our interaction.

"I didn't have to manipulate anyone into doing that," he assures me. "But anyway, what I was doing when I was that age doesn't matter because I was thirteen, not an adult with a very specific set of goals and plans years out. Come on, Reed, you're smarter than that."

I'm doing a bad job of stating the case for Cornell. It makes sense, really. I get why my family is rooting for it, and it's mostly because I've never told them what I just told Dylan so easily.

I'll need to spend the drive home picking that realization apart.

"Harper!" James calls from across the cafeteria.

Kyle, my friend from yearbook, stands with him. His

54

wary eyes and pursed lips silently tell me that he just told James about how friendly Dylan and I have been for the past five minutes.

I groan and try to end the conversation and move away from him.

We both swipe our cards to pay for our lunches, and I've just picked up my tray again when James approaches.

Damn him and his long runner's legs.

James is all smiles for me, but it's not genuine. This fakeness is almost as abrasive as Dylan's everyday personality.

Worse, he puts an arm around me. It's a gesture that he's done thousands of times before, but it's different at this moment, like he's marking his territory.

"All good here?" James asks me the question, but he keeps his eyes on Dylan.

"What's it to you?" Dylan snaps at the same time I say, "Fine."

Cue unnecessary testosterone surges.

James is still likely mad from yesterday's practice, and he's more than happy to use me as an excuse to start a bickering match with Dylan.

Dylan, of course, is just himself.

He's always calm yet ready for a confrontation, and James looks like he's about to pop a blood vessel.

My head bobs from side to side, waiting for one of them to draw the first blood.

Verbally, of course.

The only one who has resorted to violence in their feud, ironically enough, is me.

Competition in the athletic setting has been a good

outlet for them both, but now, they have a reason to interact when they're not attempting to outrun each other.

Before it can go any further, I diffuse the situation, wanting to prevent anything before it actually happens.

I refuse to be caught in the crossfire of some petty schoolyard argument.

"You both are idiots," I tell them.

I go off to find a table by myself, but I'm not surprised when James eventually sits down beside me and quietly sulks.

5

Driving is freedom.

It's only the first day of carting myself around, and I'm annoyed that I didn't do this sooner.

Complete control over the music is one thing, but it's nice to be able to do whatever and go wherever I want. After practice, James is usually too exhausted to grab food or hang out anywhere outside of our houses, but I'm always wound up after school.

I tried to make up for my attitude yesterday in the year-book office by complimenting everyone's work.

Chrissy, our staff photographer, walked me through some of the pictures she took at an art club meeting last week, and they weren't completely subpar. Brandon wrote the accompanying captions, and they were the perfect balance of direct and witty. I even patiently waited for Lyla to get through her entire planned speech on her idea for the track team spread before I shot it down, as much as it pained me to do so.

We're making good progress. We're almost locked down on the fall and winter sports articles, and the writers are gathering everything we need for the spring sports now that their seasons have started. After that, we'll tackle the features and tie up any loose ends.

It's satisfying to be on track and overseeing so many moving parts, and I already know this is good practice for any college publications I can get to agree to let a freshman join the staff of.

Checking one thing after another off my to-do list feels good.

I smile when I open the door to Books & Beans, my favorite bookstore and coffee shop in town.

Marie, the owner, greets me with an enthusiastic smile. "Your usual?" she asks.

I always wanted to be one of those people who had a *usual* somewhere, and Marie was only too happy to oblige when I told her this on my first visit.

Through trial and error, we figured out the perfect combination of chai tea, two shakes of cinnamon, a shot of espresso, and a generous coverage of whipped cream. It's spicy, rich, and sweet all at the same time.

"Yes, please," I say.

Sometimes she lets me hop behind the counter to help her make it, but there's another customer waiting behind me, so I simply watch her work.

Marie's hands move quickly over the machines with finesse.

I know she's been on her feet since early this morning, but she still looks so put together. Her light blonde hair is styled in some sort of chignon, a word I only know from reading regency romance novels, and she's probably the only woman in our town who can pull off black lipstick, sleeves of tattoos, and a baggy velvet dress.

Fashion isn't my thing. It's not just because I spend so much time in my school uniform; I just don't have an eye for it. I don't know how to mismatch prints or pull off hats or even wear eyeshadow.

If I didn't have to wear somewhat formal clothing with my school's logo on it every day, I'd probably wear the same style of jeans and plain shirts, which is why I've learned to admire and appreciate style without actually having it myself.

I toss my hair up in a high, messy bun before I accept my drink.

"Big study day?" Marie asks.

She knows I focus better without my mane of hair falling in my face.

"Physics test tomorrow," I explain. "I don't think she's going to grade this one on a curve, so I need all the extra study time I can get."

I don't mention that I usually am the one who sets the curve. It's great when an eighty percent then turns into a one hundred percent, but without it, I could do some damage to my semester grade. Which would impact my GPA and potentially dethrone me from being valedictorian, then it could impact scholarships and—

That's why I study, obsess, and plan.

"This will help." She slides a giant chocolate chip cookie wrapped in plastic across the counter. "It's on me for good luck."

Books and movies celebrate big grand gestures, but I prefer the little acts of kindness in everyday life.

"You're the best, Marie," I tell her. "Truly, you're a gift to me and this town and the world."

She laughs and eyes me. "Something's different about you today, Harper."

"It's the earrings," I tell her, gently flicking them with my fingers. "Stolen from Audrey."

The lotus earrings are the physical manifestation of something I feel deeper within me, like I'm on the cusp of becoming the next, better version of myself.

"Maybe that's it," she says.

I pay and thank her, then snag a table by the window, wishing I could bottle up the scent of books and coffee in this place. Marie would make a fortune if she figured out a way to do that.

Not that she's hurting for business. I watch other customers come in and out of the shop as I settle in. I dip a chunk of cookie into my *usual* before I chew it down.

It's warm, melty, and just what I need to power through an hour of studying.

I'm a little jittery when the caffeine hits, so I focus that energy on getting lost in a flurry of notecards, highlighters, and my textbook.

My school, of course, would prefer students to operate completely online, but I avoid my computer at all costs. It's slow and heavy, and I set my own study habits long enough ago for this to be my preferred way of working, anyway.

I guess I'm a little old-fashioned, but there's something romantic about writing something with ink in my hand.

The downside, of course, is the inevitable hand cramps,

but it's a good sign that reminds me it's time to call it quits. I clean up and wave goodbye to Marie, who insists on sending me home with another cookie.

I eat it in three bites as I drive.

"Another Italian night?" I call out when I unlock the front door of my house.

I could smell the basil and garlic from outside, and even though I ate many calories of desserts thanks to Marie, I need something substantial to soak up the coffee.

"Oh, hey," James says.

My mom laughs at whatever he said before I arrived.

He dutifully sets the table with a set of our everyday plates. They all have chips in them because Audrey is as clumsy as she is beautiful, and my mom gave up on having nice dishware a long time ago.

"It's lasagna night," James explains with a full genuine grin.

I already know this, of course, but he's excited because it's his favorite meal.

I might be biased, but my mom makes it best. It's one of those meals that tastes like home, and no restaurant can come close to replicating that. He definitely agrees.

James's parents are really strict in general, but when it comes to dieting, it's on another level entirely.

They encourage him to track his macronutrients, calories, and many other things I don't bother understanding. He follows it enough to keep him in incredible running shape, but whenever he wants to dig through a pantry with processed snack food or have a meal that's not ninety percent vegetables, he shows up at my house.

It's just so normal to have him here that I can't help but

smile as he tries to find four matching forks in the silver-ware drawer.

"What's the occasion?" I ask.

"Nothing special," my mom answers, pulling everything out of the oven.

My mouth waters at how good the homemade garlic bread looks.

"Not true," James says. "The favorite child is here, and he gets his way."

It's a long-running gag in our family that James wants to be number one on my parents' list of children. He and my dad are super close, bonding over things I don't have any interest in, like baseball and other forms of athleticism, and my mom always looks at him with pride.

I think most days James dethrones me from the top spot.

It goes without saying that Audrey and her bag—a full-sized checked bag, not a small carry-on—of problems is at the bottom. If she were here, she'd be arguing about how being the firstborn somehow influences her favor.

I'd indulge her but know she's wrong.

"You're all my favorites," my mom insists.

It's the line she always delivers.

"Not possible," I say.

"I love you all the same."

I roll my eyes. "But you like us all differently. I think we, honestly, should break down and create a point system or star chart or something."

"Sure, if you want tangible proof of how you're not in first place for the first time in your life," James says.

I finish filling the water glasses. "Yeah right."

"You have home field advantage and everything, so there's really no excuse other than how great I am."

"Stop bickering and sit," my mom orders, gesturing to our usual seats.

We oblige, but our verbal spat turns into trying to get the best parts of each dish on the table.

The crispiest end piece of the lasagna.

The helping of salad with the most cheese.

The gooiest part of the oversized garlic bread.

My mom ignores this behavior by focusing on taking a long sip of wine. "Have you two thought about what you want to do for your birthday this year?"

"Anything involving matching outfits," James jokes.

"Nope." I shoot it down immediately. "Not happening."

"But I got served this advertisement of matching underwear—"

I glare at him, effectively cutting him off.

I glance up at the many pictures of us on the walls where we are, in fact, wearing matching outfits. We stopped acting like twins and wearing matching outfits around our eighth birthday, but we've still always shared our parties. Usually, it's just family, but occasionally, James has had a girlfriend and Audrey has had a boyfriend come along.

"I was thinking it might be fun for H and me to do a roadtrip on our own," he suggests. "Maybe an early trip up to Cornell? That way we could go do all of those rites of passage eighteen year olds are supposed to do."

"Like buy lottery tickets?" I ask innocently.

"Well, definitely not cigarettes," my mom balks.

James mouths *PORN!* to me when she's focused on her plate, but she still shuts the entire idea down.

"It's one of the last birthdays we'll all get to spend together. Who knows what you'll be doing next summer. Audrey might stay up at school to pick up another minor, and Harper will be busy with her internship at the Press."

"Don't jinx it," I jump in.

She sighs. "I just want eighteen to be a special one."

"I thought it was *our* birthday," I say seriously, but there's an undercurrent of humor in my tone.

"Yes, it is the day that *I* gave birth to you, so I get to be a part of the celebration."

"You're not James's mother," I argue.

"A matter of time," she laughs.

I roll my eyes and shove a huge forkful of lasagna in my mouth. It's still a little too hot, so I blow hot air out of my mouth until my mom nudges the glass of ice water into my grasp.

James clears his throat. "Well, if it's nice outside, maybe we could rent a boat for the day? Harper loved that sight-seeing boat tour we did in seventh grade around the city. It'd be pretty cool to do that with just us."

His thoughtfulness is surprising. "That could be fun," I admit. "I'll do some research on it this weekend if you want, Mom."

"Sounds good," she says, smiling at the both of us before she takes another sip of wine.

We fall into light planning and easy conversation for the rest of dinner, minus when James and I fight over the middle of the garlic bread. My mom plays referee and hacks away at it as evenly as possible to split but makes us both groan and laugh when she steals the best bite for herself.

My dad gets home only to immediately launch into a conversation with James about when it will be warm enough to go golfing together next.

Of course, like they always do when the topic of conversation is on this sport, my dad tells the story of how he took me to a driving range and I wound up hitting a ball backward, breaking the glass window on the vending machine.

Even though he's heard the story one hundred times, James still thinks it's hilarious.

I stab my plate with a fork, but I honestly don't mind the laughter at my expense.

It's nice to have this comfort of sharing memories, and James enjoys it just as much as I do.

He fits into my life and my family so easily. Years of nothing but time together means that I don't have to worry about how he's going to act in front of my parents or if I'm paying enough attention to him.

Not like at Homecoming when Finn followed me around the entire night. I should have expected it given the fact that he didn't know anyone at my school aside from me, but it was more of a chore than it was enjoyable.

Tonight is a good reminder of how much I love James and am grateful to have him as my best friend.

If Dylan were here, he'd probably be polite enough but cooler than my parents had come to expect from a teenage boy sitting at the dinner table.

My dad addresses James as "son" more often than he uses his actual name, and I try to imagine the look on

Dylan's face if he did that while putting a hand on his shoulder. His eyes would probably bug out from the affection and human contact.

I snort out loud at the thought.

When my parents and James stop their conversation to eye me, I realize what I've been doing.

I've been imagining how Dylan Archer fits into my life.

The revelation is a little jarring. He and I have had three mostly polite conversations, but I'm already visualizing a scenario of him at my dinner table?

For once, I wish I could turn off the need to solve problems and click things together—especially where they don't belong.

Dylan and I are like puzzle pieces that seem like they might fit at a glance but absolutely do not when you look at the details.

He does not belong with me, in my neighborhood, or in my thoughts outside of our English class. This arrangement is temporary, but if I'm not careful in how I proceed, I could really damage things with James.

I blame it on my brain, creating one of those plans and sets of worries that will never come to fruition, but it still puts me in a sour mood for the rest of dinner.

After we clean up, James and I sprawl out on my bedroom floor with ice cream bars. He shoots curious glances at me that I ignore as I stare at the small television in my room.

From my side eye, I can see the tension in his shoulders, and I know him well enough to understand that he's trying to suss me out. He's replaying all of our interactions for the past forty-eight hours in an attempt to figure out what's on my mind.

I try to come up with a topic of conversation to deflect him, but with my pensive silence, he covered all the usual topics at dinner with my parents.

All I can do is sit, lick the chocolate as it melts down my fingers, and wait for him to speak up.

"Is something happening with you and Dylan Archer I should know about?" James finally asks.

And there it is.

I don't want to be deceptive, but it'd be embarrassing to tell him the entire truth.

Oh, you know, James, just fraternizing with the enemy, and in exchange for helping Dylan get his English grade up, he's keeping my complicated feelings for you a secret.

"I'm tutoring him," I say. "He's struggling in our English class."

"Dylan Archer is asking someone for help?" His skepticism is clear.

I shrug. "I guess he's really desperate."

"Huh." He chews on his popsicle stick and eyes me suspiciously.

I pretend to be fascinated with whatever food competition show James put on.

"It's just that Serena seemed really mad today," he says.

"Oh really?" I try to sound disinterested.

"Yeah, she waited for him after practice. They had a huge argument in the parking lot, and your name came up multiple times." James pauses to chuckle, clearly pleased with Dylan's hardship. "But by the time I drove off, they seemed back to normal, though. I mean, you know how they are."

I do know exactly how they are.

Just as passionate in fighting as they are making up— although usually one is verbal and the other is physical.

My stomach clenches, and I force my frown to stay neutral.

I've let my guard down with Dylan far too early in the process of whatever we're doing together.

If I'm disappointed by this news now, I can only imagine what it will be like when we start spending serious amounts of time together, and I start reading too much into everything he says.

I can't let myself be vulnerable with him; I need to be a fortress of emotion.

My skin will be a stone-cold barrier to protect my precious insides, no matter how much I want to break down and let him in.

He's not a project. I have to remind myself of that. He's a difficult person, not an assignment or inanimate object that needs to be put back together. I need to focus on the *actual* work.

"Are you sure that's all that's going on?" He says the words slowly, as if he's waiting for me to crack and gush out with some emotion toward Dylan.

I'm sure he's hoping for anger but expects heartbreak, but I just smile, shrug, and ask if he wants to watch a documentary before he has to head back home.

6

"So, I heard you officially convinced the dean to change the graduation ceremony," James says as he pulls his ankle up, stretching out his quad.

"Where'd you hear that?" I ask him.

As the assumed valedictorian, I've had a few meetings with the dean and a handful of school board members to plan the graduation ceremony. I've campaigned in each one of them against me making a speech, trying different tactics to justify why it was unnecessary.

Finally, at my argument of it being inappropriate for one student to speak for hundreds, they relented, saying it would give time back to announce each student and their assumed college and plans after graduating.

I agreed immediately, but I selfishly spent the rest of the meeting imagining myself saying "Columbia" on stage instead of "Cornell."

Our letters of acceptance or rejection are due to arrive

any day now. Even though it costs extra mileage and gas, I drive home every day to check the mailbox before driving back out to Books & Beans.

Today, I didn't get the chance because my yearbook meeting ran long, and I needed to get to the track before James's first race.

I managed my time too well, though, because now I have to stand here and watch him stretch.

"Kyle told me about it. Apparently the school board had to approve it, and you know his mom is—"

"The administrator, I know," I tell him. "I was there."

The nepotism in this school system is unbelievable. I'm just glad I haven't had the honor of meeting Dylan's dad. I barely held my ground with Dylan himself, and I couldn't imagine a version of him that had thirty years' more experience of sneering and being judgmental.

"Why didn't you tell me?" James asks.

"Because you'd try to talk me out of it," I answer him honestly.

James thrives on attention and an audience, and he doesn't understand that it's actually my worst nightmare. I'm confident in many things, but public speaking makes me want to pass out.

I much prefer putting my opinions into writing and hiding behind it that way.

James chuckles. "Look, if you're that stressed about writing a graduation speech on top of your essay for the Press, why don't you just use the same one for both?"

"It's not that I'm stressed. There are a million reasons why I should not give a speech, but it would also be entirely inappropriate for me to spend ten minutes of our graduation ceremony talking about my own personal growth when it's supposed to be a celebration of the entire graduating class."

I rant to him until I run out of breath.

He laughs at my attitude, and I huff in response. It's cold enough where I can see the air expel from my mouth.

I pull my jacket tighter around me. It was supposed to be sunny today, but a cloud bank moved in this afternoon.

James loves to run when it's overcast outside, but I'm not looking forward to sitting on the metal bleachers and freezing in my tights and skirt.

Thankfully, he is only sprinting in two events today and both are toward the beginning of the meet.

He jumps up and down in quick succession, kicking his feet back to invigorate his muscles. "Oh, come on, H, I'm just trying to loosen you up."

"You're doing a terrible job," I say, but I bite back a smile.

When they're in motion, runners look incredible, but the warm-up process makes them look like baby animals testing out their legs for the first time.

I told James this once, and he was not amused.

"It's not that cold out," he says.

"You're wearing, like, eight layers," I retort, glaring at his fleece warm-up gear, then pointedly eyeing my tights.

He rubs his hands over my arms in an attempt to warm me up. I don't feel it between the layers of clothing, but it's a nice gesture.

"Well, you can put this on while I run," he says. "Maybe it will bring me good luck."

He starts pulling off his sweatshirt and sweatpants

before I can answer, but I'm grateful for the extra layers and accept them without complaint.

"Oh, cool, a free coat rack," Dylan's sharp voice says behind James.

Dylan is completely unbothered by James's glare as he strips down. They're both wearing tight shorts and Under Armour long-sleeve shirts that will keep them warm and show off their muscles while they move, and I'm not mad about it.

"I'm a helpful human, not a piece of furniture," I tell him.

Dylan gives me a mocking half-smile. "Lucky us."

I roll my eyes but hold out my arms so I can accept the extra layers of fabric.

"Remember what I said about being nice to the people who are doing you a favor," I shoot back.

"Am *I* doing *you* a favor?" Dylan drawls. "Seems like you're ill-equipped to deal with the elements."

"You admit to doing something selfless, then?"

James watches us volley back and forth until we're interrupted by the horn of the loudspeaker.

"All eight hundred meter relay runners at the start," the deep voice announces, made crackly by the speaker. "One hundred meter runners on deck."

Dylan turns and walks off toward the starting line without another word, but James pulls me into a quick hug, then plants a kiss on the side of my head before he follows.

"Good luck," I call out.

I'm not sure who it's aimed at, but James is the only one who acknowledges it.

I find a spot in the stands that's more in the middle of the crowd. Most people congregate at the finish line, but I want a good view to watch the entirety of the race from beginning to end.

A few parents wave to me, recognizing me from years of sitting in proximity, and I smile back.

I scan the crowd for the Lawsons, but James's parents are nowhere to be found. I'm like a daughter to them, and we get along really well, but I admit I'm relieved to not have to keep up small talk with them.

Instead, I wrap myself up in the inherited clothing and force myself to be interested in the events happening on the track and in the field.

As well studied as I am, I hate to admit that my minimal knowledge of the metric system is credited to staring at the track and learning what the different events mean.

Each lap around the track is four hundred meters, and it takes a little more than a minute to run.

Well, for these people. Definitely not me.

Four laps is a mile. The longest race at the meet is two miles—eight laps, which is more than three thousand meters.

Math isn't my favorite subject, so I tend just to watch people during these meets.

My eyes move back toward the starting line where James and Dylan stand actively ignoring each other.

It's funny to see them stand in close proximity and wearing their matching uniforms, but it's clear from my vantage point just how different they are.

I always associate Dylan with a darker, edgier persona,

but he's actually the fairer, taller, and leaner one of the two. His blond hair is slicked back a bit today, no doubt to keep it out of his eyes while he runs.

James, of course, has the physique that I've studied for years, but I give myself a few minutes of shameless public gawking to notice how he has really filled out. I guess he does get some use out of that weight set and bench in his garage when I'm not paying attention.

As the other race finishes up, the two of them, seemingly in unison, get prepared for theirs. They've both already stretched, but they move their limbs quickly again through the motions to shake out nerves.

Spikes are checked to ensure they're within regulation before they adjust the starting blocks and get in position.

This is the shortest race at the meet at one hundred meters, one-fourth of a lap.

They'll start and finish within eleven seconds, and I'll hold my breath the entire time.

James is in lane one today, and Dylan's in lane three.

The middle lanes are ideal for the other events because of how each runner takes the curve of the track, but for this one, it apparently doesn't make too much of a difference. I've come by this information somewhat reluctantly, but over the years of watching, I was forced to learn a few things.

The voice over the loudspeaker starts again, announcing the winner of the last race and the start of this one. The chatter around me dies down as the focus shifts to the lanes in front of us.

This is my favorite part of the whole event.

It's the stillness before the start.

The one final breath before the jump.

The serenity before the chaos.

When James runs, he transforms from something light and airy into pure ferocity. It's an interesting transformation, like he's shifting into an alter-ego to tap into a more competitive part of himself.

But when the starter says, "Ready," my eyes are drawn to Dylan.

He rolls his shoulders to release that tension he wears like armor, as if he's giving permission for his body to shed its sharpness.

Only he's not changing into something else. Dylan's himself to a fault, but he's revealing something deeper in himself, exposing a new layer to everyone who watches him.

I doubt anyone notices or appreciates it like I do at this moment.

The muscles in his body are more defined when he drops a knee onto the track, like they were made to support this action and nothing else.

"Set."

His hips lift in the air, and he effortlessly holds his weight in his arms and core. His feet press against the starting block, ready to launch.

He closes his eyes, just for a second, and then he waits.

I wish I knew what was going through his head at this exact moment.

The entire stadium is quiet, waiting for the showdown that's going to last mere seconds. The anticipation is worth the energy surge in its purest form.

"Go" is announced by the deafening pop from the starting gun.

They're off.

The angle at how they pop up means the first few strides are taken with their heads down, fixed toward the ground until physics gives them the leverage to fixate toward the finish line.

His legs propel him forward in an even cadence, but his arms are mere accessories as he widens his stride.

The pace at which his body moves makes me believe that he's untouchable.

He's right in front of me, but somehow, he's on another plane of existence.

I finally breathe when the blurs cross the finish line.

Times are checked, and James comes away from the group with a huge grin on his face.

They both walk toward the field encircled in the track to catch their breath while a few of their teammates offer congratulations on taking the top two spots. Sometimes I'm so focused on the individual outcomes that I forget that track and field is actually a team sport.

"You know, you almost seem disappointed for someone whose best friend just kicked some serious ass."

Brandon sits beside me all nonchalantly, but his words are heavy.

"I don't know what you're talking about." I say this with as much seriousness as I can muster, but I've been told that I have a terrible poker face.

James waves at me, and I stick my hand out from the layers of fabric momentarily to return the gesture.

"Right," Brandon says.

We both watch Serena saunter over and offer Dylan a sip of her Gatorade, but I turn my head to Brandon to distract myself from whatever that outcome is.

"Do you come to a lot of these?" I ask Brandon.

Aside from being Dylan's best friend, Brandon is new to the yearbook staff, so I feel like I have an obligation to be cordial.

"Not really," he says. "I'm usually too busy, but Lyla's trying to rope me into helping her with the track spread, so I felt I should get reacquainted with it."

"Are you saying that just to get on my good side?" I ask.

"Am I on your bad side?"

Brandon's personality reminds me so much of Dylan's—guarded and sarcastic comments with exceptionally formal words for our age group. It's like they're close to speaking in formal British English while still having American accents.

Maybe it's a rich people thing.

"Not yet," I admit.

Brandon watches the long jump event with feigned interest before he says, "So, Dylan tells me you actually sit here and do homework sometimes instead of watching the events. Do you not find them entertaining?"

I have to blink at the admission that Dylan actually said something to another human, especially one in his inner circle, about me.

Brandon's gaze is on my features like he's expecting me to give something away when I speak.

"Dylan who?"

He smirks, and I know I've said the right thing.

I don't think boys like Brandon and Dylan do friendships like normal people. I have to speak in riddles to earn approval and keep up the conversation, and honestly, it's kind of fun.

I adjust the sweatshirt on my lap, tracing the white block letters of ARCHER that sits across my thighs. "Is that the tall blond one?"

"Don't you mean the devastatingly gorgeous heir to the Archer fortune who is trying to avoid getting felt up by his ex-girlfriend and catch the attention of his English tutor?"

I keep my eyes locked on Brandon's brown ones, refusing to show enough interest in Dylan to see if he's telling the truth.

"Why would a boy like that need help with anything?" I ask.

"It's the same question I've been asking," Brandon mutters.

"But, hypothetically, if I were aware of who you were speaking of, wouldn't it be odd for his best friend to be speaking to the best friend of his mortal enemy?"

He considers this. "Hypothetically, we'd be carbon neutral," Brandon decides. "Although we're pulled into the bad emissions from time to time, we plant enough trees to offset."

"Actually, I think we're both signing up to kill a bunch of trees. I don't know how many of them are used to create a fifty-page yearbook, multiplied by everyone who buys one, but it can't possibly be good."

"Guess we'll have to find another way to stop global warming."

I smile. "Works for me."

We watch the next few events in comfortable silence, and I'm thrilled to have a companion who finds this sport just as dull as I do.

A few parents chat me up and ask about my post-graduation plans, but I deflect by introducing them to Brandon or babbling on about how buried I am in schoolwork at the moment.

Brandon stands when the four-hundred-meter race is announced.

"You're leaving before the best part," I tell him somewhat bitterly. "The one hundred meter is interesting, but it's over so fast. This one is more complex. I mean, there are curves and plans for pacing and everything. You can't miss it."

"I'm just going for a quick smoke break," he explains. "Want to come?"

I'm somewhat flattered by this offer, but it's also repulsive. "Do people still smoke cigarettes these days? I thought that all of the studies, commercials, and scientific proof about the link to cancer nearly obliterated that entire industry."

"Who says it's cigarettes?" Brandon poses, shoving his hands in his pockets.

I don't necessarily want to understand what he is implying.

"I'll pass," I say. "Thanks, though."

Brandon shrugs, and I'm left to watch the race alone.

It's a full lap around the track, so their lanes actually have an impact on the angle that they run. James has spent hours explaining to me the endurance needed to maintain that fast of a speed for that length of time and how he changes his strides when he is on the curves versus running on the straight lines.

This time around, I'm overly invested in the outcome of this race, trying to decide who is going to be more insufferable to deal with if James wins the second one of the day.

In the end, Dylan beats him by a full two seconds, which is nothing in the normal span of time, but in the sprinting world, it's a huge margin.

Brandon doesn't return to our spot, so I wave bye to some of the parents I chatted with and make my way down to the track.

"Congratulations," I say to Dylan as I reluctantly hand over his outerwear.

It's getting colder by the second, and I can't wait to be in the safety of my car once again.

"Bring a scarf next time, Reed," is all he says to me as he shrugs everything back on.

I ignore the attitude. "We're still on for tonight?"

"Did I send you a letter with my regrets or otherwise change our plans?" Dylan asks rhetorically. "Then yes."

Nearly a week after we had our verbal handshake, we're finally having our first work session.

I offered to get started last week or over the weekend, but Dylan kindly reminded me that some people actually have things to do that aren't school related.

He's pretty grouchy for someone who just set a school record.

I'm about to call him out for being a jerk, but James does it for me.

"Watch your mouth, Archer," James says almost lazily as he nabs the sweatshirt from my hands.

Dylan rolls his eyes, but he doesn't back away from us.

I think he's waiting to see how I'm going to react to the tension between them. Or maybe he just doesn't care.

Like a coward, I keep my mouth shut and let James lean on me so he can step into his sweats. He leaves his arm possessively around my shoulders when he's finished and speaks to me directly.

"My parents want to take us out to dinner after the meet," James says.

"I was wondering why they didn't show," I admit. "I looked for them in the stands."

"They had to work late tonight and wanted to make it up with Mexican food."

It's a typical move by James's parents, trying to butter him up when they're feeling guilty. Although James has admitted to me at least one dozen times that he doesn't mind it when it's just me in the stands, they don't know that.

"I do love guacamole," Dylan says, earning a glare from James. "But Reed and I have plans."

James looks at me in disbelief, even more so when I confirm it.

"AP English stuff," I say before I turn to Dylan. "I'll meet you at the car, okay? It's the—"

"I know which one it is."

James grips my shoulder like he doesn't want to let me go.

"I'll see you tomorrow," I tell him as I remove his hand

and head toward the parking lot. "Tell your parents I said hello."

"Harper," James calls as I'm walking away. "Be careful, okay?"

Dylan laughs. "Oh, for Christ's sake, Lawson. We're doing an English assignment, not fooling around in her backseat."

James shoves him before he storms off.

I immediately pull out my phone to text Dylan.

Was that really necessary?

The text is unreturned, of course. He's probably in the showers or getting cool down instructions from one of his coaches.

I wish I had my usual from Marie to help warm me up, but I decide to expend the gas from my car to heat up the interior while I replay my conversation with Brandon over in my head.

I can't help but wonder if he had some ulterior motive for joining the yearbook staff—and for sitting next to me today—but all the reasons I come up with are embarrassingly self indulgent.

Dylan knocks on my window, pulling me from my psychoanalyzing.

"Yes, Reed, it was necessary," he says after he slides into the passenger's seat. "You two making googly eyes at each other is exhausting."

I can't help but chuckle. "Did you just say 'googly eyes' out loud?"

He glares at me.

"I don't think it had anything to do with me, really," I tell him.

"It had everything to do with you," Dylan insists, voice low.

I freeze.

A horrible new rationalization surfaces in my mind.

This whole thing is a setup. It's some scheme to get close to me. To mess with my mind and do some mind trick to get me to turn against James or divulge sensitive information in order to screw him over.

I mean, within a day of this agreement, I readily offered up James's dream college. What if Dylan's father has a friend in admissions over there? It's not a stretch by any means because of his position on the school board. Surely he has a big network in academia.

"Dylan, I need you to be completely honest with me," I say slowly. "Are you specifically asking for my help just to annoy James? Is this some sort of mind game or way to get one over on him? I mean, there are so many other students in our class with less of a conflict and more patience, but you specifically sought me out. Why?"

He sinks back in the seat, as if it's his only comfort at this moment, and sighs. "You're such a contradiction, Reed, and it's stressing me out."

I balk. "What? Me? Stressing *you* out? That's ridiculous."

"How can someone with so much brains and determination be this shattered all the time?" Dylan asks, verbally throwing his arms up into the air. "It has to be exhausting to walk around with your heart open and your ego ready to get wounded."

I chew on my bottom lip. As much as I want to keep up the fortress of not letting him get to me, this truth does.

"It is pretty exhausting," I admit.

My own honesty is surprising and a little involuntary.

Dylan actually looks a little impressed at my candor, but the words settle between us unanswered.

I clear my throat and pivot the conversation away from me. "Do you have the packet from the short story unit?"

He digs in his bag and hands it over almost immediately.

I flip through it. "This is half finished, Dylan...and half-assed."

He shrugs in response, which irritates me to my core.

"Is it a reading comprehension issue or a laziness one?" I ask. "Are you purposely trying not to do this?"

"I told you I wouldn't make you do the work," he says.

I sigh. "Okay, let's start with the first question on the T.S. Eliot poem."

To get into damage repair mode, I pull back my hair, eliciting a gasp from Dylan.

"What?" I look in the rearview mirror to make sure I didn't draw on my face with my pen or do something that warranted that reaction.

"Reed, are those earrings regulation?"

He's mocking me.

Of course.

I roll my eyes. "Does your father make you recite the dress code every night before dinner or something?"

"Only on Tuesdays," he deadpans before he admits the truth. "I've heard enough girls complaining about it to know that those are not permitted. Harper Reed breaking the rules. Wow. Never thought I'd see the day."

I slip them from my ears and drop them in the center console. "Happy now?" I ask.

"Not particularly," Dylan says.

"Not my problem," I tell him.

We spend the next half hour going through every question in the packet.

Once we get in a groove, it's easy, almost too easy. Dylan argues with me over the answers, claiming that multiple choice questions are too deceiving. We banter back and forth about the most direct answers to the short answer sections.

"If we stick to this schedule of doing one or two of the makeup assignments a day on top of the regular assignments, you should be caught up right around spring break. Have you already read the first five chapters of *Brave New World* for this week?"

"Sure," he says, but it's clear that he stopped listening to me a while ago.

I smack his arm, and he refocuses on me.

"Are you even listening to me?"

"Mostly."

For someone who asked for my help, he seems generally unmotivated to actually accept it.

"What is your deal, Archer?" I ask him. "I've got all of this stuff and stress piled up on my plate, trying to plan for a future, and I'm dragging you along with this as best I can, but you seem unbothered by everything that doesn't involve simply doing the bare minimum."

"What's wrong with that?"

I sputter. "There are so many things wrong with that, I don't even know where to begin."

He laughs. "Live a little, Reed. You're going to burn out and go gray by the time you're nineteen if you keep this up."

"Get out of the car," is the only response I can give him.

Thankfully, he obeys.

7

The next day in Independent Study, I decide to focus on the essay.

I've been researching different ways to be productive, so I decide to try the method of no distractions for an entire period. Solely focusing on what I need to do and nothing else.

Maybe facing the challenge head on is just what I need.

I toss my hair up, flip to a blank page in my notebook, and pull out one of my favorite pens. With this setup, I'm ready to take on the world.

James, alternatively, is playing some mindless farming game on his phone. He doesn't realize it, but he keeps tapping on my chair with his foot in an uneven rhythm.

I scoot my chair back, just out of reach from him, and readjust my focus on the page. I write my name at the top, as if that will help put me in the mood to write a personal essay.

The other times I've attempted to do this, I went in

with the intention of writing the best thing I've ever written, being flowery but succinct with words, being witty without trying too hard.

Essentially, trying to write perfection before I've even decided what it is that I want to say.

This go-round, I just write with no expectation, starting with interesting and possibly pivotal moments in my life.

When we moved next to the Lawsons while I was in utero.

When Audrey went off to kindergarten.

When my dad got a promotion, we got a new refrigerator with an ice machine in it.

When James won Homecoming king.

And they're all absolutely pathetic.

More importantly, all of these events aren't even really mine—they're other people's moments that I was present for or benefitted from.

I stop myself, wondering if I can use that to possibly write about how influential and supportive I am. A real sideline supporter and champion for my loved ones.

But that's not true either.

James doesn't run faster because I'm there. He just does it, and I witness it.

I scratch at the paper with my pen in frustration.

"What's wrong, H?" James asks in a low voice.

I move back toward him, letting our knees knock.

"My essay," I say with a frown. "It somehow simultaneously sucks and doesn't exist."

He takes my notebook from me, and I'm glad that the ink has smeared to a point where he wouldn't be able to make out the words even if he wanted to.

"Why are you beating yourself up about this?" James asks. "You're putting way too much pressure on yourself, and you're going to drive yourself crazy, and it's just going to be more of this."

He squeezes my knee under the table.

"Let's do something fun this weekend and get your mind off it."

"Okay," I agree because I'm willing to try anything at this point. "Maybe a walk in North Park if it's not too cold? Would be good to get out without the distractions."

"Or the movies if it is?" James suggests. "There's a new horror film that—"

"Not a chance."

The last time James talked me into going to see a scary movie, I had to avert my eyes for half the film, and I was so on edge I couldn't even eat the popcorn.

"We'll find middle ground. Just know that I can absolutely not sit through another chick flick. I don't care if it helps you write the most amazing essay of your life. I draw the line at another sappy thing that's going to make you cry."

"Fine," I sigh and spend the rest of the period watching him tend to the carrots on his digital farm.

In AP English, Dylan is actually cordial to me.

We have to partner up to write the parameters of a dystopian world we would potentially create if we were writing a novel, and I can't help but gush to him about how I think it's a great assignment as we're doing it.

I love the thought exercise behind world building, and when the bell rings, I'm trying to figure out how I can do other writing projects like that.

"Reed," Dylan says, pulling me back to reality.

He falls in beside me as we walk to the cafeteria. I'm in a bubble of project excitement, and I'd be more than happy to sit by myself and churn all throughout lunch.

"Is your normally packed social calendar clear tonight?"

I stop walking and eye him skeptically. "Potentially. Why?"

"That was a joke, Reed," he says. "Of course your social calendar is open. I just watched you write 'research world-building exercises' in the to-do list section of your planner."

I cross my arms on my chest. "Stop making fun of me and get to the point."

"My plans were canceled for tonight, which means I have extra time to get harassed by you about schoolwork."

I lay it on thick. "Wow, someone actually gave up the opportunity to hang out with you on a Friday night?"

"Apparently," he says sourly.

"Did you get stood up?"

He eyes me. "Getting stood up means you go to the agreed location and the other person doesn't show. Have you ever actually been on a date before, Reed?"

I roll my eyes. "Is this whole 'mocking me' thing going to continue on throughout the evening?"

"We'll see," he says. "Let's meet up after practice."

He doesn't give me time to respond before he's off again.

In the cafeteria, I pick at my lunch and engage with James and some of his friends on the track team.

My eyes keep flickering over to where Dylan and Brandon sit.

They're deep in conversation, and for all I know, they could be plotting to take over the world. When I notice that Serena, who is sitting at the end of my table, keeps her gaze fixed there, too, I force myself to talk to James for the rest of the period.

Later, after Marie hands me over my usual at Books & Beans, I text Dylan to let him know where he can find me if he still wants to do English work. We didn't actually solidify our plans, so I'm trying to leave it open-ended.

I can be nonchalant.

I think?

I planned to do some research on my phone for the world-building exercises and check out other dystopian books in the store, but when I see an older couple sitting at the next table, they take up my attention.

And it's not because they're doing something extraordinary. In fact, they probably are boring to the average patron, but I'm simultaneously boring, average, and intrigued, so it works.

Their hands are joined across the table, a physical connection established between them while they occupy their own worlds. He sips his coffee and works on a cross-word puzzle. She does the first spine-breaking read of one of my favorite Elizabeth Gilbert books.

My brain won't stop creating all sorts of scenarios for their backstory, and I want to learn more about them and understand how one goes from what I am now to who they are together.

It's something that no matter how much I read about, I don't understand it. And that bothers me.

It pains me to interrupt their scene, but I want to.

"Excuse me," I say.

They both look at me expectantly, but there's warmth to it.

"I was wondering if you like that book so far?"

The woman smiles. "Oh, yes," she says brightly. "It's a little more scandalous than I expected, but I'm enjoying it."

We chat about where she's at in the book, and her husband encourages me to pull my chair over.

"No use craning your neck," he mumbles.

Marie catches my eye as I join them, and it's a silent *See? Something is different about you!*

I soon find out that Gary and Linda Dailey live in Youngstown, Ohio, but make monthly trips across state lines to visit family. They spent the morning babysitting their granddaughter and wanted to get a quick rest and coffee break before hopping back on the interstate.

I ask them at least a dozen questions about their lives and retirement. They, in turn, are curious about my schooling, interests, and plans for next year.

It's so easy for me to be honest with them, these practical strangers, about how my heart is set on Columbia. I'm glad I am because they gush about the trips they've taken to New York City over the years, and I live vicariously through them.

As I write down my fifth restaurant recommendation from them in my planner, the front door chimes.

Linda's eyes go wide, and I turn my attention to see Dylan watching me curiously.

"Oh, he's a cute one," Linda says a little too loudly to me.

I laugh and wave him over.

"Short practice?" I ask him.

The ends of his hair are still wet.

He nods. "The win yesterday bought us a break, apparently." His hands hang by his side, and his gaze flickers to the table. "Aren't you going to introduce me?"

"Oh, right, uh, Gary, Linda, this is Dylan."

They all shake hands, and I fill them both in on surface-level details of each other.

There's a brief moment of awkwardness when I run out of things to say.

"Well, it's probably time for us to head out," Linda says. "But I have your email address now, so I'll be sending you the other restaurants on my list."

"I would appreciate it so much, thank you," I tell her, hugging them both before they leave.

"It was so nice to meet you," Gary says.

"Drive safely!"

With a wave, they're out the door, and Dylan's eyes are back on me.

"You just met them?" he asks flatly.

"Yes," I say, noticing that he's not moving to sit or order at the counter. "Are we going somewhere?"

He nods. "Yep. Let's go."

"You're driving." I drain the remainder of my chai and toss it.

I head to the counter, leaning over to call out to Marie, who is wrangling some paperwork in the back. "Marie, is it okay if I leave my car here for a little while?" I ask her.

"Of course," she calls. "Heading out already? Thought it'd be a late night for you."

"I'll try to swing back before closing to see what cookies you have left," I promise.

She laughs. "Works for me."

I turn back to Dylan, whose expression is indescribable. "Lead on, then."

When we're in his sleek SUV, which has a logo I don't even recognize, he finally lets out a half-chuckle, half-sigh. "So, as if it's not ridiculous enough that you spend your Friday night doing more schoolwork, you decide to chat up the oldest people on the planet?"

"Hey! We had a great conversation." My defense is weak, but I press on. "Were you not the one making fun of me for my social calendar? Well, look at that, I made new friends. Two of them. It was fun."

He pulls out of the parking lot. "I think your 'fun' barometer is off, Reed. Talking to old people is not fun. Going out and doing wild and reckless stuff is how teenagers are supposed to have fun."

"Is that what you had planned with your mystery date before you got stood up?" I ask curiously. "Wild and reckless stuff?"

He exhales and taps on the steering wheel as we idle at a red light. "By your standards maybe, but not by mine."

"Coyness is not my favorite one of your traits," I tell him.

"I didn't realize you had favorite things about me," he says lightly.

That is a subject I do not want to touch, so I change it. "You don't listen to music when you drive?" I ask.

He presses a few buttons on the fancy touch screen. "I

think you can set your phone up for Bluetooth if you want to play something."

"You're willingly letting me choose?" I ask.

"As long as it's nothing too terrible, I can cope."

"Wow, James barely ever lets me pick the music..."

"Another thing I have over him, I suppose."

I don't respond, but I choose one of Modest Mouse's first singles, and it immediately gets rejected by him.

"Oh god, that's the worst song," he tells me.

"You're the worst song," I defend lamely, and it earns me a grunt of annoyance.

I press next on shuffle, and I'm happy to find out that Interpol's "Untitled" seems agreeable by his standards.

"Are you going to tell me where we're going?" I ask.

He turns down one of the back roads that leads to the big shopping mall in town. "If I do, are you going to be thirty percent less annoying?"

"I'll consider it."

"Good tactic, Reed. Don't agree to anything you're not one hundred percent certain of. I approve."

I sigh. "So are you going to tell me or not?"

"It's not so much where we are going but what we are doing."

"Too cryptic, Archer."

"I'm just not sure it will be as *fun* for you as spending Friday night with two seventy-year-olds."

"I don't know why you're harping on this. I realize most of your free time is spent playing mind games with Serena or whoever else you're fooling around with these days, but if you actually sit down and have a conversation with people, especially those who are older than you, it's actually worthwhile. They've lived lives almost four times as long as mine, experienced new places, and I learned a lot from talking to them in a short amount of time."

"Everything's a learning opportunity for you, isn't it?" He shakes his head, like it's painful to come to this understanding, then grins devilishly. "Well, then, I know what your next lesson can be."

"A lesson? I'm more of a self-guided learner."

He presses on. "And it's the perfect way to repay you. I've decided that I can't accept your help without giving you something in return."

"I don't want—"

"Money or your secret to get out, I know," he says. "But it has come to my attention that you're in desperate need of help with something."

"Not another hair joke," I whine.

"I was actually thinking we should do something about your confidence."

"Confidence?" I repeat. "I don't think I have a problem with that."

"Being a know-it-all isn't exactly what we're going for, Reed."

"But being an arrogant prick is, I guess?"

He shakes his head in irritation as we pull into the parking lot. "It's a well-practiced art that comes with time, but it should be worth it."

I don't like where this is going, but I follow him inside the mall silently.

We're standing at the edge of the big indoor cafeteria, and Dylan explains that he wants me to approach a guy our age and ask him out.

He pointed out that I just did a very similar thing with old people, but I've been arguing against this exercise for the past ten minutes.

"Shouldn't I be getting a big makeover montage before I do this?" I ask him. "That's how it's done in the movies, at least."

He rolls his eyes. "This isn't some crappy made-for-TV movie, Reed. This is your life."

"Well, I don't see how *this* is going to help. I think you are doing this for your amusement, not for my benefit."

The smell of the various food stalls is actually making my stomach growl loud enough that I just want to get this over with so I can gorge myself with Chinese food.

The stall on the far side has my favorite spring rolls in the entire world. James always makes a disgusted face when I mix every available sauce together and dip them in, but I think the mixture of flavors and spices is delicious.

"Confidence comes from within, Reed. I know my ruggedly handsome exterior is a distraction, but it's my winning personality that keeps me drowning in women," he says smugly.

"You know, I thought you were doing me a big favor with this, but you're actually really enjoying seeing me so miserable, aren't you?"

He levels with me. "I had no idea where we were going when I picked you up, but did you know that?"

"No," I admit.

"Confidence," he says.

"You go first," I insist. "Show me how it's done."

"What a cop-out. You've already seen my magic in

action. You're just stalling. Go ahead, pick your target, or I'll do it for you."

I find humor in his veiled threat, but I still take in as many people as I can in the food court.

There are a few couples on dates, people eating alone, children and exhausted parents, groups of teenagers and...

Familiar inky black hair catches my attention.

A few tables are pushed together to accommodate the group's size, and I recognize James, obviously, Kyle, Serena, and a few others from our school. The table is covered in wrappers and trays, indicating they're almost done.

I watch as the vacant seat beside James is filled by a smiling Lyla, who was James's first kiss. Half of our third period class saw it happen in the hallway, and afterward, he told me that he hated the way her lip gloss stuck to his mouth.

It was part of the reason I was a lip balm only girl.

Dylan is oblivious to my disappointment as James puts his arm around Lyla. It's familiar, like he has done to me so many times, but she falls into him in a way I never allowed myself to.

Worse, she whispers something in his ear before he turns and kisses her gently on the lips.

I turn my back to the scene.

"Oh, come on, Reed," Dylan chides me. "It's not really that difficult."

He continues talking, but my mind is in overdrive.

I'm aware that I don't have ownership over James, no matter what hope I have for us in the future. This group could have casually bumped into each other after school and practice, but from my view, it seemed...intentional. Like they were all deliberately paired off.

Dylan Archer, of all people, sought me out while my best friend went out with a group of people and didn't send me a text to invite me to join them.

Worse, he's apparently *dating* someone and didn't tell me, his lifelong best friend.

The tears pool in my eyes, a tangible marker of how hurt I am, and I will them not to fall down my face. Not here and certainly not in front of Dylan.

"I'm not doing this," I tell him.

Thankfully, my voice hasn't revealed the emotion clotting in my throat.

Dylan follows me as I walk briskly through the doors and across the parking lot. It's one of the few times in my life when I actually consider running of my own accord, but I'm embarrassed by the thought of it.

By sheer will, I'm at least somewhat composed when we arrive back at his car, but the door doesn't budge when I lift the handle.

I turn to him now that I'm certain the tears have disappeared completely, going back to wherever they belong.

"Open it," I nearly bark at Dylan.

"No," he says lightly, leaning against the car frame, as if he has nothing but time.

I try the handle again, jerking it violently, but it doesn't open.

"You can't control everything, Reed."

"Did giving you a black eye in fourth grade not get the point across? You're not going to bully me into doing whatever you want."

I hold my ground on the fact that this exercise was only an effort to make me feel humiliated because the actual cause of my humiliation is too much to bear. I can't even imagine trying to explain it to him.

"I never thought I'd see the day when Harper Reed backs down from a challenge."

"It's not a challenge, Dylan," I snap. "I don't need you to work on my confidence or anything else you think needs to improve. Unlike you, I don't hate myself. I actually like who I am. Now, stop goading me and unlock the damn door."

He's too amused by my frustration. "Did you just curse at me?"

"Archer, come on. Let's get out of here."

The last thing I need is for the group to finish up and find us out here, together and alone on a Friday night.

"Why is this a touchy subject for you?" Dylan asks, genuinely curious.

I've been more open with Dylan than I have with my own family, but this goes deeper than college choices; it's an intentional omission of the truth from someone I've trusted with years of my life.

I expect deception and half-truths from guys like Dylan and Brandon, but James? He's supposed to be different.

"You have gone out on dates before, yeah?"

Dylan's still hung up on this topic.

"Wasn't there that guy you went to Homecoming with? Some sort of fish name."

I glare at him. "Finn."

He laughs. "Did he kiss like a fish, too?"

He kind of did, honestly, and the memory makes me frown.

"Oh no, Reed," he groans. "Don't tell me...please tell me you've been kissed."

"Of course I have," I say without hesitation.

Innocent.

Cute.

Innocent and cute.

James's words flash in my mind, and it's hard to juxtapose that with the image of him and Lyla together. What else has he been keeping from me that makes me seem so virtuous in comparison?

That question doesn't make me angry. Actually, it makes me curious.

There are many things in this life that I haven't experienced. Innocent things like the type of affection that Gary and Linda Dailey share, but other things, too. The kind of things that make me reconsider the intensity of Dylan's eyes on mine.

My instincts scream for me to run, but all I can do is press against the closed car door.

"I'm not talking about a peck on the cheek, Reed," he says, his voice gravelly. "I'm talking about letting go of everything, completely and thoroughly."

The air around us somehow changes with his tone.

It's like I'm watching him again on the track preparing to sprint. He's deliberate in even the slightest of movement. His chin tilts slightly downward. His chest expands.

He's using every piece of himself to get my attention, and it's working.

My palms press against the smooth exterior of his car. I'm frozen, hanging on every single word he says.

"Have you ever been so lost in someone else that you nearly forget yourself?"

I swallow. The sound is loud in my ears. He's so close now; I wonder if it is in his, too.

My encyclopedic mind can't recall being on the receiving end of this type of look, like I'm staring down the barrel of a loaded gun. He has his hand on the grip, waiting to see if I'm brave enough to pull the trigger or if I'll insist on flipping the safety.

"Everything ceases to exist except the warmth and the friction…" He trails off.

My heart pounds in my chest as he puts one hand on my hip and moves the other up, twisting his fingertips in the curls that he has ridiculed for years.

His hands are rough, not in texture, but in movement.

I gasp when he tugs at me, but as he leans downward, I'm the one who closes the gap between us.

I've seen his lips pulled into a hard sneer more times than I can count, so I'm surprised that they're soft and warm when pressed against mine. I don't get to appreciate the sensation for long, though, because I drown in everything else when he kisses me back.

He's greedy and relentless in his kiss, like I'm withholding something that he so desperately wants, even though I'm matching his pace.

Any worry or nervousness that surfaces about his infinitely more experience is pushed away when I hear the low moan in his throat and he presses even harder against me. I lock my arms around his neck and hold on for the ride.

His mouth moves briefly from my mouth to kiss at my neck. I inhale gulps of cold air, but the shiver that goes through me is all because of him.

Just as I'm falling deeper into it, he cruelly withdraws himself.

"And that's how it's done," he sneers.

I blink rapidly, taking in his almost inhuman coldness.

I'm not even hurt that I've so clearly failed whatever lesson he wants to teach me. I just don't understand how someone kisses like *that* and feels nothing.

Surely even he can't be this heartless.

My shaking hand touches his stomach, feeling the hard lines of muscles beneath his button down, and I drag my fingers up to his chest.

His heart pounds, just like mine. You can fake a lot of things in life, but I don't think that's one of them.

At first glance, he seems appalled by my touch, but his eyes soften.

Something deep in my brain clicks.

He doesn't know how to accept affection.

I'm so full of emotion that it drives almost every single thing I do in life, but Dylan's calculated in a different way. We both have deep faults, but I've experienced tenderness many times in my life.

Has Dylan ever held someone's hand just because? Or been hugged in excitement?

Given what I know about his personality and the way he handles his friendships and relationships, I can't picture it.

But he should experience it.

Just like he decided I should know what it feels like to be manipulated by someone in complete control, I'm going to show him what it's like to be adored without strings attached.

He watches my hand as I move it from his chest up to his collar, but when I trace my thumb along the hard line of his jaw, then the little scar I'm responsible for on his cheek, his eyes bore into mine.

Somehow, out of everything we just did, this feels the most intimate.

Dylan Archer's tongue was just in my mouth, but the caress of one of my fingers on his bottom lip is something he has to feel with his eyes open.

I think he's too shocked to do anything other than let me kiss him again.

So I do it.

I move slowly on purpose, wanting to be slow and gentle in contrast to the bruising kiss he pressed against my lips.

It's a completely different kiss, but once we get going, it's hard to stop.

The passion is like a punch in the gut. I'm trying to defend myself against it, but it still breaks through. My entire body feels the repercussions of it.

I hope he feels that way, too.

As if he's responding to my inner monologue, he moves my forearms to his shoulder, granting himself unobstructed access to wrap his arms around my waist. I'm pulled up on my toes and crushed into his chest.

And it's good.

Too good, actually, considering that we're in a crowded

parking lot, and it's not even completely dark outside yet. I remember where we are, what we're doing, and who exactly we both are.

I deliberately slow the pace to a stop.

My eyes open.

I'm breathless, but he's something else entirely.

Out of all the books and words contained in my brain, I don't have one that perfectly describes Dylan Archer at this moment. In fact, all descriptions seem inadequate.

"I-I'm." I don't know what I'm trying to stutter out, but he finally releases his hold on me.

He steps back and just observes my state, as if he needs some explanation for whatever just happened.

I feel disheveled from head to toe, but I'm pretty sure the only indicators of what just happened between us are my swollen lips and pounding heart.

Without a word, he digs his keys out of his pocket and unlocks the doors. We get in, then we sit in silence for a beat.

I'm complicit in what just happened, but I'm also stunned and unable to come up with anything to say next.

He turns the key and throws the gear in reverse to high-tail it out of the spot, but just as fast as he started, he stops. He slams on the brakes hard enough that the seat belt cuts into my neck.

I look over my shoulder to see the slow-moving throng of our classmates wander to their respective cars.

They don't recognize Dylan's SUV, and it's not light enough outside anymore where they can pick us out from the front seats.

There's a tall light in the parking lot that casts a spotlight on each person as they walk past. When Lyla and James walk by holding hands, I force my gaze away, turning back to the front windshield.

The burn of betrayal is still palpable in my throat, but I already know that I'm going to give James the opportunity to explain himself.

He gets off easy, but it's me and Dylan who have it tough.

I clear my throat. "You're taking me back to my car?" I ask.

"Yep," he says simply.

I turn, realizing he's been watching me.

"Do you still want to go do homework somewhere?" I ask him.

His jaw ticks, and he seems, out of every emotion, angry. He doesn't bother to respond; he just glares at me. I take it as a no.

I try to find the right way to talk to him on the ride back to Books & Beans.

"Do you want to talk about it?" is what I come up with.

"Talk about what, Reed?" Dylan's voice is neutral, but I think he is straining himself to keep it that way.

I flinch. "What we...the parking lot."

"Nothing of consequence happened in that parking lot. Understand? If it wasn't you, I would have been some-where else with someone else tonight. And things would have progressed far more quickly and easily than it did back there."

My mouth drops open at the severity of his words.

"Okay," is all I can say to him before I step out of the car.

He zooms out of the parking lot, and I understand that while his response was honest, in the most gutting way possible, it was also self-preservation.

I think back to the conversation we had in the library; the day he first asked for my help.

"You think the world is all about using people, Dylan. It's not."

"You say 'using' like it's a bad thing."

He thinks I'm just as bad as he is.

And I don't know if he'll trust me to show him that I'm not.

I feign happiness as Marie slides a few cookies my way, then I spend the rest of the night wondering if I should update my life plans or burn them all to hell.

8

I've set myself up at our dining room table.

It's the one that only gets used at Christmas or the occasional dinner party my parents have with a small group of friends, which always includes James's parents. All other times, it collects papers, delivery boxes, and anything else that doesn't really have a dedicated spot somewhere else in our house.

Today, I decide, it's where I'm going to sit and write my essay.

Or rather, where I'm going to sit and stare at the blank document that should be my essay.

I breathe a sigh of relief when James comes in the house through the side door after an hour of nothingness.

"H, you here?"

"Dining room," I call back and shut my laptop, effectively throwing in the towel for the day.

James makes a quick pit stop in the kitchen for a bag of

chips, which he reluctantly shares with me when I hold out my hand.

Honestly, he's a welcome distraction.

"So, what will it be?" James asks, sitting in the chair beside me and propping his feet up on the one across from us. "Walk in North Park or movies?"

"Shoes off the furniture," I tell him for the millionth time in our lives.

I don't know where he got this habit from. Not only does it gross me out that he's putting his filthy sneakers where we sit to eat, but the chair pads are white.

When I own a house someday, all the furniture is going to have to be in a dark fabric.

I stop myself because it's another little thing I'm planning in my life around James, and after last night, I feel a little strange about it.

"Let's do something different today," I suggest.

He raises an eyebrow. "Different? You sure you don't just want to go to the movies?"

"I checked, and nothing looks good for both of us," I lie quickly.

For the most part, I usually love going to see new releases with him, especially when we drive to the big theater downtown with the leather seats that recline. We usually raise the armrest and make a little comfortable nest for the two of us, which hardly seems appropriate given the fact that he is most definitely with Lyla.

But also, I just don't want to sit beside James in a dark movie theater for two hours.

"Surely there are plenty of things in this city that neither of us has done before?" I say.

He hasn't totally bought into this idea yet. "Like what? The science center or something?"

That would require planning and coercion on my part, so I come up with something else off the top of my head.

"Here," I say, pulling up a map of Pittsburgh on my phone. "Now close your eyes and drop your finger on the screen. Wherever it lands is where we spend the day."

"You're sure about this?"

"Just do it," I snap and move it closer to him.

He lands on Shadyside. "Not the worst place I could have picked."

It's actually a beautiful part of the city.

I've driven through it a few times with my parents, but I haven't spent much time wandering through the streets and stores. Since it's sunny, we decide to walk around and get lost for the day.

We stop in random antique shops, boutiques, and paper stores that seem to carry far more items than actual paper. James talks me into buying a new hat and scarf set, which I desperately need, and then we window shop a few restaurants before we stop into a small diner for lunch.

"This has been nice," I say to him.

"Yeah," he agrees, tracing the rim on his mug. "It feels like we spend all this time together, but at this point, it's a little blurry."

I know what he means.

We've spent so many years of our lives on my bedroom floor and at the kitchen table that it's kind of hard to pick out any specific moments. But it's the summation of them all, I think, that means something.

"It's good to do something new," I admit.

"And think of all the new things we'll experience at Cornell next year," he says with a smile. "College parties, new friends, different places."

I hum noncommittally and take a long sip of my coffee.

"Many more days like this." The words are almost wistful coming from his mouth, like he's dreaming up a future he's really looking forward to.

He slings his arm around the back of my chair, causing me to shoot upward.

I've spent years loving every little touch and gesture from him. Everything about him, really, but something about last night cracked the rose-colored glasses I've been wearing my entire life.

"James," I sigh.

"Uh oh."

"What?"

"Whenever you say my name like that, it's because you're going to scold me or ask a question you really are dreading," he explains. "My predictable H."

Innocent.

Cute.

Predictable.

I grind my teeth and prepare to stab him with my words. "So, you're dating Lyla again?"

His eyebrows practically shoot up to his hairline. "How'd you hear about that?" he asks.

"Does it matter?" I bite back.

He shrugs. "It happened last night, actually. We decided to kind of take it slow. You know, she just broke up with that exchange student a few weeks ago. We started talking during Calculus and then it happened."

112

It seems reasonable enough, minus the fact that he left out the part about going out with her last night.

Who knows when he would have told me if I hadn't asked him directly.

"Are you mad?" James's voice has a strange pout to it.

I don't know how I would have reacted if he sprung this information on me casually. So as much as it stung, it was almost better to see it for myself and rip the Band-Aid off in private.

This isn't the first time that James has had a girlfriend, and it likely wouldn't be the last.

"Of course not," I say. "Well, I'm not mad that you have a girlfriend, but I don't know why you didn't tell me."

He takes one of my hands in his. "I don't know why either," he admits.

I focus on swallowing the dregs of my coffee.

"Let's go wander around a little more," I suggest. "I think I saw an art gallery next door that looked interesting."

James groans. "I thought you promised to never drag me to a museum again."

During our sophomore year, we went to one of the art museums downtown, and he made it clear how boring and uninteresting it was, making fun of the pieces instead of appreciating them.

Only a few of his jokes were funny.

"It's a *gallery*," I emphasize. "It's different."

I drag him by the hand until we cross the threshold.

We're greeted at the front desk and handed booklets with a little more detail on the collection. We're informed that instead of one showing by one artist, the current collection is from many different artists around the city, and all profits from the sales will be donated to an art charity.

It's not an overly large space, but there's a lot in it.

Thankfully, James and I dropped our hold on each other when we started mulling around, but I can practically feel his impatience radiating toward me from a few paintings over.

I take my time to appreciate just how different each item is. The pieces are exquisite, and it makes me wish I knew more about art than I do.

Aside from a sideline appreciation, I can't offer much else.

I stop at a painting that is perhaps the most unique piece I've ever laid eyes on—it's a monstrosity, maybe eight feet tall and a few feet wider.

It's a depiction of a human heart. It's styled like street art, but it's crafted beautifully. I can't tell if the layers are actually spray paint or if the artist was so meticulous about the coloring that it somehow just looks like it.

The main cavity of the heart is like a shiny red ruby, reflecting brilliantly with the light at even the slightest movement of my head. The ventricles have an industrial feel to them, as if they're drain pipes and gears without being actually and obviously depicted that way.

I wish I could zoom in on the image to see how many pixels of gray, white, and blue are incorporated into the black abyss of the background, which contrasts the rest of the painting so brutally.

I take a step back, wanting to appreciate the work at a different angle, and I gasp when I realize that the heart itself, so powerful at first glance, is actually quite damaged. I can see the bruising along the bottom and dotted along the right ventricle.

My fingers itch to touch it, to feel the pain that the artist bravely put on display in this work and to somehow help it heal. Although I'm not a gallery regular, I know that's not permitted.

Art is meant to be admired and appreciated in a way that isn't disturbed by the chaos of humans, whether it be the oils from our hands or the clumsiness in damaging something so precious.

No matter how deeply you think you connect with a piece, it's not yours to claim.

Unless you have the cash for it, I suppose.

I flip through the program. While most pieces have details on the artist and a paragraph of notes about the piece, its origins, and a few other details, all I get on this one is:

The Wait of the Human Heart
Yarra DeLinch
Create Date and Location Undisclosed

"This thing is seven thousand dollars?" James exclaims in my ear.

I was so lost in the painting I didn't hear him approach or notice he was looking over my shoulder.

"What does it even mean?"

He's looking at the same canvas, materials, lines, and work that I am, but we're somehow seeing something completely different.

"I think it's up for interpretation," I tell him, purposely being a little coy.

James blinks and rubs the back of his neck. "Seems pretty straightforward to me. Someone got bored and decided to go through a whole lot of paint."

I look around, thankful that no one else can hear how crass and disrespectful he's being.

"Just because you don't necessarily understand something doesn't mean you can't appreciate its beauty," I scold as quietly as I can.

Every second I stand in front of this painting, I'm more intrigued.

James shifts on his feet, a slight movement that voices his impatience with my dawdling without him even having to open his mouth.

It's distracting me enough that I can't fall wholeheartedly into the feelings this painting evokes, so I give in.

"Come on," I sigh. "We can go."

He perks up instantly.

I look at the painting one more time, longingly, before we head out.

Things are back to normal on the ride home and even more so when we arrive. My mom greets us when he pulls up and tries to get him to come over for dinner, but he blushes and says he has plans.

For the rest of the weekend, it's just me, my parents, my homework, and my non-existent essay. Despite how it started, overall it's a good weekend—especially when my mom burns the heck out of her casserole on Sunday night and we order pizza instead.

Occasionally, I wonder what Dylan's plans are for the

weekend, and I even consider texting him to make sure he was staying on top of his study schedule I created for him, but I ultimately decide I'd rather face him in person tomorrow.

Scolding over text messages isn't a great look for anyone.

I'm antsy through the first few classes in the morning. I don't think I take a full inhale until I step in Miss Delway's room and see Dylan sitting there with the same bored look on his face he usually has.

He's cordial and a little distant, spending most of his time ignoring my attempts to stray from anything that's not directly related to the assignment we're working on.

It continues like this for the rest of the week.

I watch him at every opportunity I can. But it's limited to class, lunch, and his away meet at a nearby school on Wednesday.

On Thursday, I follow him to the cafeteria and finally snap when he idles at the salad bar. "Are you just going to keep ignoring me, or are we going to get back to whatever we were doing pre-parking lot?"

A smirk tugs at the corner of his mouth, but he seems very interested in the salad dressing options in front of him. "How about tonight?"

I open my mouth and close it again. I hadn't expected his outright agreement.

"Okay," I agree. "Books & Beans after practice?"

"No practice today."

"Really?"

He cocks an eyebrow like he's surprised I don't already have this information. "Just at-home stretching.

Coach's reward after slaughtering the other team yesterday."

"Oh."

"But I left my computer at home," Dylan adds. "Let's just go there to do the work."

"Go to your house?" I stutter.

He looks at me like I'm a complete idiot. "Is that an issue?"

"No," I say quickly as I reel.

He's inviting me over to his house. Only it's not just a house; it's a *mansion*.

I don't know which one is specifically his, but it's in a ritzy area of the city, and they all are triple the size of mine.

Some of them even have guest houses and swimming pools, which is such a weird concept to me considering that my own yard barely exists. It's basically three feet of grass that breaks up the space between my house and James's. What does a person need a guesthouse for, anyway, when the actual house has six bedrooms?

Maybe I'll find out tonight.

9

There's something intimidating about the stature and size of the Archer family home.

I can't decide if it's the way the driveway seems to go on forever, taunting me with a never-ending paved road, or if it's the dark exterior that feels a little too much like something from a horror movie, but it all makes me a little nervous.

If a house could exemplify Dylan Archer and his personality, this is it.

He opens the door before I can knock, and I can't help but gawk at the interior. It's all high ceilings and marble, and the furniture is all ornate and beautifully crafted.

It's actual, livable art.

I'm afraid to touch anything.

It's clear I, with my frayed backpack and wild hair, do not belong in an immaculate place like this.

I clutch my belongings to my chest as he leads me down the hall and up the stairs to his bedroom. It takes, maybe, twelve big steps to get from my front door to my room at my house, but I swear we walk for at least five minutes before I step into his bedroom.

Correction: I step into his *suite*.

Because there's a full sitting room and multiple doors that are open wide enough that I can see the corner of his bed, the tile of a bathroom, and the entrance of a massive walk-in closet. This might actually be bigger than the entire second floor of my house.

"Are you going to just stand there?" Dylan asks, not bothering to look up from his laptop as he speaks.

He's already made himself comfortable on the expansive leather couch, so I take a deep, calming breath before I sink in beside him.

I pull out my dinosaur of a computer, planner, schoolbooks, and the study schedule, delicately placing each one on the sleek coffee table. I focus on organizing them neatly because I'm still feeling a little jittery and out of place.

"I see you've decided to move in, Reed," Dylan says, watching me restack my books.

There's a playfulness in his voice where there's usually a sharpness.

I can't decide if he genuinely thinks what I'm doing is funny or if he can sense how on edge I am and he's attempting to reassure me. The latter seems completely impossible, so I'm just going to assume my organizational skills are hilarious.

Before I can overanalyze that one sentence any longer, he adjusts his posture so that his computer rests comfortably on his knees. He angles them, and his sleek MacBook, toward me so I can look at his work.

I frown at his progress. "You're behind schedule," I tell him, gesturing to the study schedule I created. "You were supposed to have this argumentative essay done on Monday."

He rolls his eyes. "Such a stickler for your own made-up rules."

"They're not rules. It's how I'm helping you get back on track." I stop and take a breath to refocus. "Okay, so let's see, at least you've chosen a poem. 'The History Teacher' is a good choice, and Billy Collins is one of my favorites. What stance are you taking?"

"That he is a horrible teacher."

"Because?" I ask, trying to make headway on his messy outline.

"He lies about history and sugarcoats events in an attempt to make the children less cruel."

"You don't think there's something noble about that?" I argue, glancing at him once more to see his reaction.

He's in full debate mode with a ghost of a smile and a gleam in his eye. "He's supposed to be an educator, not a storyteller."

"You don't think there's anything morally okay with stretching the truth?"

I, myself, think it's circumstantially okay.

Like when Audrey asks me my opinion about an outfit that I think exposes way too much skin for me, but she is radiant in it. My telling the truth would only hurt her feelings because I'm holding her to my own set of standards.

But James not telling me about his "taking things slow" with Lyla...that still feels like a betrayal. On some level, I'm aware it's not my business, but when you set the standard of telling someone things, then abruptly stop, it hurts.

"Not necessarily," he answers. "In this case, it has no effect on the outcome except that he's defying his obligation to tell the truth and not spread misinformation."

"You're acting like he's a journalist or a scientist not a children's school teacher. I agree, there should be standards, but every single sentence—"

"If we don't hold the people responsible for teaching the events correctly, how can we ever expect people to learn from mistakes? Textbooks are notoriously slanted to an exclusive narrative, but how can we trust anything we've learned if those responsible for teaching us are revising truths on whims?"

I snort. "I'm not sure I agree. Life is cruel enough, and as long as the message gets across, I'm not sure the details are important. We spent years learning bits of history from Egyptian times, but what do we recall? A few names maybe? But if we learned the truth of every single bloody battle, would it really have any benefit? Or would it rationalize more bloodshed and war in our young, impressionable minds?"

"I guess that's for your own essay, not mine."

"It was," I admit. "It was exactly what I said when I turned in this assignment when it was actually due in January."

Dylan sighs. "Let me guess, you got an A plus for your brilliant argument."

I feel the redness creep over my cheeks. "Actually an A minus. She warned me she was going to start docking points if I continued to double the required word count, but I didn't believe she actually would."

"And after your entire pro-teacher stance and everything? Wow. You must really be driving her crazy."

"Well, at least she seems to like you just fine," I huff.

It's maddening because even though he hasn't put in the work by any means, he's got a safety net that I definitely do not have.

"Maybe she'll let you donate those words to me."

"I might have to. This outline doesn't even make sense. You're burying your argument in the third paragraph." I pause. "How did you get this far in high school without me?"

He shrugs his shoulders. "Cheating."

I gasp, completely horrified.

"I'm kidding. Now tell me the foolproof Harper Reed method to absolutely crushing an essay. But actually within the word count."

I jump right into problem-solving and planning mode. "First, let's fix the outline. It doesn't have to be pretty, but it does need to follow the rubric if you want to actually pass the class."

I'm trying to use a condescending voice, but I can't maintain it because I am happy someone is actually asking me about the way I do things.

"Then I recommend you write your intro and conclusion sections to ensure—"

"Doesn't it make more sense to start at the beginning and work through it?"

This arrangement is starting to feel more one-sided by

the minute. Not only is he borrowing my brain but my patience as well.

"I've found it's best to write them both together because the conclusion is supposed to reiterate the introduction, not necessarily add to the paper." My voice is a few notes higher because I'm trying to maintain the false politeness between the two of us. "You could accidentally put new information in, which will cost you points."

"We certainly wouldn't want that," Dylan mocks.

I shove the laptop back toward him so that he can work on his paper. I pick up my own computer, deciding I'll use the time to try my method on my personal essay for the Press.

Once he has given me the internet password and I've approved his outline, we work quietly side by side. He's typing quickly and easily, and I'm actually jealous at the sound of the quick keystrokes. If the Press would have asked me for an argumentative paper instead of a personal essay, I would be keeping up with him just fine.

I click away from the blank white document and decide to seek out other essays online. Maybe they'll help guide me into finding my own voice somehow.

I quickly discover that there are so many good examples and writers attached to them that I feel stupid for the ineptitude to tell my own story.

When I'm looking at stuff that has already been written, it seems so easy, like it's the most obvious thing in the entire world to be able to do.

But the stories I read are full of conflict, childhood complications, and obstacles that the writers overcame.

What do I have to share?

Nothing.

I frown.

"Is your *computer* making that noise?" Dylan asks.

The overworking of the fan is white noise to me, but given that Dylan is using a sleek Apple product instead of an eight-year-old Dell, he's probably used to being able to have multiple windows open at once without consequence.

"Sorry," I mutter, closing everything until it's just me and the blank document once more.

Dylan's interest in what I'm doing doesn't fade once the noise of the fan does. "I thought you were all caught up on your work and then some?"

"Correct."

"So, what are you working on?"

"A personal essay."

"For what?"

I swallow, deciding it's just better to get it all out at once than deal with his interrogation on my half-truths. "The Pittsburgh Press has this writing contest open to high school seniors. I'm trying to win so I can intern with them next summer. I have to write a personal essay, but I'm struggling with it."

"I would too if I was trying to use a computer from the nineties," he retorts immediately.

I glare at the boy who has probably never touched anything secondhand in his life. "It's my sister's old one. It works just fine for what I need it to do."

"Except work in peace, apparently," Dylan says, eyes narrowing on my laptop. "No wonder you can't get it done."

I wish it were that simple. Blaming technology instead of the resistance I can't break through in my head.

As much as Dylan challenges me, he does have a habit of spurring me into action. He doesn't have time for nonsense, and despite my best judgment, I'm wondering if he can actually *help me* with this.

I turn and tuck my legs underneath me so I can see the way he reacts to my next set of words.

"Well, it's not exactly that," I say lightly, although it guts me to admit to him. "I'm struggling with what to write about."

His eyebrow ticks up. "You're lecturing me on writing a paper, and you can't even write an essay?"

That was not the reaction I was hoping for. "It's not that simple," I start.

He wrinkles his nose and attempts to mimic me. "First, you start with the outline…"

"Funny."

I shouldn't have put any hope in getting anything other than mockery from Dylan Archer.

"You have a plan for everything then, Reed?" he asks. "Lining up internships before you even graduate high school. Already figuring out your entire career and life at age seventeen."

I'm definitely a little abnormal with how I've mapped out the entirety of my life all the way to the end, but I doubt there's a person in our grade who hasn't thought about their own future well into their twenties.

But Dylan could be an exception.

"You haven't put any thought whatsoever into what you're going to be doing post-college?" I ask him.

He has no biting retort other than mumbling, "Touché," before he goes back to his own work.

Dylan's advice, if I could even call it that, was to actually just follow my own process. I sigh, resigning to try it out.

I start by writing out what should exist, an introductory paragraph, first point, etc., until I reach the conclusion. It took me thirty seconds to do, but I already feel so much better, like I'm at least starting to put the work in instead of sitting around groaning about it.

And it's then I have to mentally give credit to Dylan.

It's hard to admit you're failing and even more difficult to ask someone you barely tolerate for help.

There's something endearing about his serious expression as he focuses on the words on the screen in front of him. His fingers fly, letting the thoughts flow through his hands, and I watch the movements, mesmerized slightly.

His blazer, a key component of our school uniform, is nowhere to be found. His sleeves are rolled up, and I'm fascinated by his hands and wrists, especially when he moves up a hand to brush his hair to the side.

My phone vibrates on the table, breaking me out of the gratuitous staring I've been doing.

It's James. *Can I come over?*

I'm not home. All he would have to do is look outside his window and see my car isn't parked in the street. We don't have standing plans, but it's almost dinnertime, so maybe he's hoping to get away from his parents.

Normally, though, he'd just walk in the side door and make himself at home in the kitchen instead of texting me, so I send him another message. *Are you okay?*

Yeah. The typing bubbles don't stop until he sends his next message. *You at B&B?*

No. I glance at Dylan and the lines slicing across his forehead in concentration. *Helping Dylan.*

I wait a few minutes for James to respond, but he doesn't. I twiddle my thumbs, considering texting him again, but I don't.

"There," Dylan says with a note of resolve. "Done."

"With the first draft," I say, unable to suppress my grin.

He groans. "If you're going to make me do more of this, I'm going to need food first."

Whenever James and I do homework, it's usually either at one of our kitchen tables or bedroom floors, and we're often surrounded by more bags of chips and cookies than books.

I once proclaimed that the sugar and fat combination is a magical recipe for productivity, but somehow, I doubt Dylan would share that sentiment.

Everything about his house is more formal than what I'm used to, so I shouldn't be surprised when he leads me to the kitchen and I see a woman who has to be Dylan's mother chatting with another woman who seems to be a professional chef *cooking their dinner*. But I am.

I'm screaming internally at the luxury.

"Dylan, you didn't tell me we were having company," his mother says sharply to him.

I suck in a breath, fully prepared to start groveling and apologizing for being in Dylan's room without her permission. I'm sure that most moms wouldn't want some strange girl lounging on their son's couch.

Dylan ignores her comment and heads straight for the

refrigerator. Of course, it's the size of a closet and totally packed with brand name drinks, yogurt, snacks, and everything else I could imagine.

He takes out two bottles of water, handing me one, which I accept with a smile.

Bottled water.

In a house.

When there are *two* sinks in this kitchen and exposed shelves with rows of glassware.

I fiddle with the label and take in his mother's polite expression. It looks eerily similar to the one Dylan fixes when he's trying to keep his composure.

"My son has forgotten his social graces," she laughs warmly. "I'm Abigail."

She extends a hand, and I shake it.

"I'm Harper Reed. It's so nice to meet you, Mrs. Archer."

"Seems someone knows how to do a proper introduction," she scolds and playfully snaps a hand towel at him.

Dylan rolls his eyes. "We're in the middle of homework."

"Homework," she repeats, taking in my appearance. "Is that what kids are calling it these days?"

Dylan's eyes take in the creases on my pants and untamed hair. "Oh no, that's how she always looks."

"I thought we agreed on no more hair jokes," I say to him quietly while I unsuccessfully try to brush through my curls with my fingers.

He shakes his head. "I never agreed to anything like that."

"We're really just doing homework, Mrs. Archer. AP

English seems like double the workload this semester," I say to Dylan with sharp eyes.

"Well, all that studying must be making you both very hungry, and Marcie is putting all the finishing touches on the first course."

First course. Where on earth am I?

"There's more than enough here for you both to join us."

Dylan twists the cap on his water bottle. "Oh no, we'll take it up—"

"Thank you, Mrs. Archer," I jump in. "I would love to."

I graciously accept before he can finish declining. I pointedly ignore Dylan's glare. He clearly was not planning on me joining in on a sit-down dinner, but it's such a good opportunity that I can't pass it up.

It's like my own personal sociological experiment, seeing and understanding where Dylan Archer came from and why he is the way he is.

"Can I help set the table?" I ask, attempting to be the gracious guest.

My mom always ends up shoving various plates and everything at James and me until we begrudgingly move everything over to the table. Filling up four water glasses is such a simple, mundane task, but for some reason, I can't stand it and always try to pass it off to James.

She regards my offer with a look of surprise. "Oh no, dear, it's all taken care of for us. Why don't you go ahead and get situated? I'll be in shortly."

Dylan begrudgingly leads me to the formal dining room.

I don't have a chance to stare at the carved archway or the art on the walls because I'm so taken aback by the table itself. If she had wanted me to set the table, I wouldn't have had a clue where to even start.

There are two plates stacked on top of each other at the individual place settings and seven pieces of silverware decorating it. I don't know how many courses a person has to eat that require that many utensils, but I'm eager to find out.

My stomach grumbles in excitement.

Dylan actually pulls out a chair for me, and I fully expect him to yank it out at the last minute so I fall onto the floor, but he doesn't.

His mother enters and hums in approval as I take my seat.

"Is Father joining us?" Dylan asks.

I pick up on the edge of nervousness in his tone, but his mother doesn't comment on it.

"It appears not," she answers coolly.

He repeats the same motion for her, and she takes her spot at the head of the table, leaving Dylan to sit across from me and scold me for the entirety of the meal.

10

The Archers are apparently well versed in the formality of the sit-down dinner and letting others serve them. The chef brings in the first course, expertly balancing three bowls between her two hands.

I inhale the rich scent of garlic and well-seasoned tomatoes. Part of me wants to just pick it up in my hands, drain it, and ask for another serving.

I watch the way Mrs. Archer uses her spoon, the one on the far right of her place setting. How she eats is almost a skill, scraping the side of the spoon lightly across the top of the soup, smoothing it along the back end of the bowl before bringing it up to her mouth.

After a few sips, she places the spoon between the bowl and one of the plates and starts to engage me in polite conversation.

She asks me about my family and school projects, and she seems to be surprisingly interested in my plans for the yearbook.

I don't hesitate to gush over what I've been working on, telling her about how the entire project plays on the Throwback Thursday trend online where each spread encompasses the feel of a sort of social media scrapbook.

"I couldn't think of a better way to encapsulate this time than by trying to be a reflection of who we are as a generation, so defined by our online presence."

"That is certainly an interesting idea," she compliments. "How did you come up with it?"

"Last summer, my mom made my sister and me clean out the attic, and we found a box of her and my dad's old yearbooks. They were pretty funny, I mean, early nineties hairstyles and whatnot. But anyway, all of the pictures were so posed and the superlatives were pretty cringey. It just seemed so overdone and corny, and I wanted to figure out a way to not be like that."

Mrs. Archer laughs. Well, it's not exactly a laugh—more of a smile with sound.

"I, for one, am grateful my mother refused allowing me to perm my hair."

If I were her mother, I probably would have refused it, too. Her blonde hair, even if it's colored that way, is absolutely gorgeous. Like a sheet of pure gold.

The last time Audrey tried to straighten my hair, it was curling up again on the first side before she even finished the other.

The chef replaces our soup bowls with salads, marking the start of the second course. It's a few pieces of shredded kale with julienned carrots, sunflower seeds, and two pieces of shrimp arranged beautifully on top. It smells divine, but I have to stop myself from swallowing it in two bites.

If the portions are this tiny, I assume we're going to be here for three hours and at least ten courses.

Mrs. Archer expertly shifts the conversation back to Dylan, asking him how Brandon is doing with whatever charity organization his parents have him volunteering with.

With the attention off of me momentarily, I get the chance to study both Archers and the interior.

Dylan's mother is so proper with every word she speaks and movement she makes, I don't know how anyone speaks to her without feeling self-conscious. Seeing her makes me understand more of Dylan, mostly how rigid and deliberate he can be.

I wonder what parts of his personality are from his father, but I'm not sure I'll get the chance to find out.

I'm taking in the beautifully decorated walls, with real light fixtures and bulbs that don't look like they've been sitting in the garage for who knows how long, and I stop at one of the art pieces on the wall.

It's not exactly like *The Wait of the Human Heart* from the gallery with James, but I think I recognize the style of layering paint and the way it makes me feel so isolated and comforted at the same time.

Even though it's about one-tenth the size and drastically more simple, it's no less powerful.

It's much longer than it is tall, and it's an expansive set of wings. I usually associate wings with angels or birds against blue or pink hues, but this work is the antithesis of that feeling. The majority of the painting is white with black slashes that are somehow violent against it.

I wait for a lull in their conversation, practically fidgeting with excitement as I do, until I get to ask Mrs. Archer, "Is that piece by Yarra DeLinch?"

She blinks, somewhat impressed by my question. "Why, yes it is. Art is also one of your interests?"

"Not really," I admit. "I definitely have an appreciation for it, but I don't think I've ever really felt like I 'got it,' if that makes sense. Well, except for this artist. I saw another work by her at a gallery in Shadyside."

"I didn't see that in your planner," Dylan says tightly, addressing me directly for the first time since we sat down.

I give him a challenging look. "I didn't realize you were studying my plans so closely."

The remnants of my salad are traded for a round cut of steak and a few potatoes.

Dylan picks up his knife and fork without breaking our eye contact. "Well, if you had let me know, we could have arranged for a private viewing."

Mrs. Archer takes in the confused expression on my face. "That gallery is one of mine, dear," she says.

"One of yours?" I ask.

"My mother has dedicated her life to the arts," Dylan explains. "Aside from running a non-profit dedicated to ensuring inner-city children are able to access music, writing, and other classes at no cost, she owns and curates a few galleries around the city."

"That's incredible." I wish I had something more eloquent to say. "I couldn't find anything about the artist online. Have you met her personally?"

"Quite a few times, but she's very reserved. Refuses to come to the gallery openings or get recognized in the public eye, much to my disappointment. This piece was a gift. It's one of the first works she did on canvas. She actually started out as a street artist but moved to canvas after she got caught defacing a billboard—"

"Mother, I doubt she is interested in the long, boring history of this," Dylan says.

"Don't interrupt me," she scolds him quickly before turning to me again. "Are you interested?"

I nod enthusiastically, then Mrs. Archer tells me more about her work, and I follow her lead through the remainder of the courses.

Both Archers eat like judges on a television food show, delicately cutting and tasting each bite while holding a fork and a knife in each hand. In my house, the side of the fork is my preferred knife, but I adapt just fine.

Mrs. Archer insists that we have dessert and coffee in the library, and I don't put up a fight at all. In fact, I'm more eager to see their collection of books than I am to hear more about Dylan's childhood, some of which I recall from our early years at school together.

The library is stunning, but it's the most cramped room I've come across so far. The walls are lined with books, and there are a number of armchairs and couches arranged on massive print rugs.

I relax enough to run my fingers along some of the spines as I read the words printed on them.

My eyes are drawn to the far corner of the room where a few books are housed in an antique display case. I gasp at some of the titles, and my hands start to shake when I see *Pride and Prejudice*.

It's three volumes in a deep red tone, and they appear to be incredibly well preserved.

"Oh my god," I cry out involuntarily. "Is this a first edition?"

I'm dying to touch these, but I know I can't. Not only would it be entirely inappropriate for me to ask to do so, but I wouldn't want to smudge them or, god forbid, damage them in some way.

It's just like the painting at the gallery. I want to feel it in my hands, to cradle everything I'm feeling, but I can't trust myself with something so precious.

Dylan is by my side, looking at the books with bored interest, as if he was glancing at today's newspaper. "Are you...okay?"

"Yes," I say, but my throat is thick.

It's incredible to think that a story written by someone who lived such a different life, more than two hundred years ago, still resonates to this day.

The chef brings in a tray of dark chocolates and coffees, and it's almost hard to move myself back over to settle into conversation again with Dylan and his mother.

I try to mimic the way Mrs. Archer wipes her mouth with the corner of her napkin *just so* and then folds it back in on itself before it drops on her lap, but I fail and end up crumpling the cloth in my lap.

Each bite of this dinner and dessert is more delicious than the one before it. I'm flattered that Mrs. Archer asked me to join them, and it was an all-around positive experience. But I can't help but still feel so damn hungry, and I'm embarrassed by it.

I don't know if I'm used to bigger portions or if I was deceived by the presentation, but I'm curious as to how Dylan, someone who runs miles and burns a ton of calories each day, could be satisfied with that meal alone. I'm not one to count calories, but I wonder if he's got a spare fridge stocked with more food in his room.

When we're finished, I thank Mrs. Archer for inviting me to dinner and accept her offer in the not-too-distant future to accompany her to one of her galleries. I barely get a chance to turn back to wave before Dylan presses his hand on my back, pushing me along to his room.

I shrug him off.

I assume he's annoyed at me for this entire charade, for weaseling myself into his personal life, and who knows what else, but when his father calls his name and I turn to look at him, I now understand what he wanted to spare me from.

Andrew Archer stands proudly at the other end of the hallway.

His spine is straight, his head is bald, and his eyes are pure aggression.

"Father," Dylan says as the elder Archer takes a few slow, deliberate steps toward us.

He doesn't say anything. Like a villain in a movie, he just moves forward and stares at the two of us.

It's an uncomfortable silence, and I don't open my mouth to break through it, unlike the brief comfort and confidence I found with Dylan's mom.

"And who's this?"

"Harper Reed," Dylan answers evenly. "We're classmates."

"Reed? Of Reed Enterprises?"

I recognize the name. It's a relatively new tech company in the city that's been raising a ton of money. Apparently, the founder is a computer prodigy of some kind.

Dylan looks at me and tilts his head toward his father, silently urging me to respond.

"No, Mr. Archer," I say quickly. "No relation to me. My parents are both accountants."

"Which firm do they own?"

"Oh, um, they don't own a firm. They both work at Peters & Richley."

I'm embarrassed by how nervous I am, but this is how these types of men are. I don't have a lot of experience with the rich and elite of Pennsylvania, but I know enough about them to understand that they love this power they hold, this silent intimidation.

His father raises his chin to stare me down with narrowed eyes before he flicks his gaze back to his son. "What happened to the other one?"

Dylan's jaw ticks.

"The Montgomery girl," he snaps, as if he needs to clarify.

"Serena and I are still friends. But Harper and I are eager to get back to our homework, if you'll excuse us."

Again, his hand hits my lower back, and this time, I will it to stay fixed to me like it's my only lifeline.

"I do not believe I dismissed you."

I can't help but swallow, and it's a loud sound.

Thankfully, Mrs. Archer steps out of the library, as if she's surprised to stumble on people in her own home.

"Hello, dear," she says, greeting her husband cordially.

She holds out her hand for him, and he kisses it, like how I would imagine someone would greet someone from the royal family in London.

Mrs. Archer and Dylan apparently have some silent conversation exchanged in a seconds-long glance because she puts her arm on her husband's bicep.

"Why are we all standing in the hallway having a conversation like uncivilized humans?" she asks. "Andrew, join me in the library, and I'll have dinner brought in for you."

I smile at Mrs. Archer one final time before Dylan and I bolt to his room.

We don't resume on the comfortable couch or even pretend to care about schoolwork at this moment because I'm processing the absolute potential monster that is his father, and he's watching me do it.

In Dylan's tight expression, I can see it all.

The harshness he experienced growing up.

The brief moments of softness offered by his mother.

His desire to flee from the family business and find life elsewhere.

The pressure he's under to succeed.

My mind, in a moment of creativity, colors between the lines, inserting every possible scenario. I'm grateful that, although he is many things, he's relatively unscathed.

Dylan's life is clean and strict. It's wrought with

formality and handshakes, like he skipped over the entire part of life where you play in the mud and eat candy until you puke, which, in my experience, is almost never worth it, but he doesn't know that. Yet.

In addition to getting him an A in English and the hell away from this place, I want to mess up Dylan's life. In a good way.

But I'm going to need to miss my weekday curfew to do it, so I fire off a text to my parents in our group chat. It's convenient because they both constantly seem to be misplacing their phones, but usually at least one of them has theirs on them.

Hey. I'll be home in a bit. Going out to dinner with a friend after homework.

My mom responds with her typical overuse of punctuation. *What friend?????*

Dylan Archer. We have English together.

Where is James????

I don't know. I'm tempted to add an eye-roll emoji, but I don't.

I need details when you get home!!!! Not too late!!! You have school tomorrow!!!

I know. Love you, Mom.

Love you!!!!!! So much!!!!

I laugh because although she's irritating at times, she's undeniably cute.

"What?" Dylan asks, his eyebrow lifting at my smile.

It's almost cruel to have to tell him how funny and sweet my mom is juxtaposed to the frigidness of his parents, so I lie to prevent more hurt, just like he advocated against earlier. But this is my decision, my argument, my renewed sense of purpose.

"Um, just something James sent."

I don't miss the way his lips tilt down a fraction.

"Hey," I say, recapturing his attention. "Any chance you're still hungry?"

11

Dylan Archer is accustomed to white table cloths, many small and manageable courses, and light chatter over a meal.

Naturally I have to take him to my favorite wing place, where a line of bikers sits on their motorcycles near the entrance, smoking cigars and laughing loudly at one another's expense.

If Dylan's uncomfortable, I don't pick up on it. His composure is intact as we sit ourselves at a table, stepping on discarded peanut shells along the way, and take in the grease-stained menu.

"What can I get ya to start with?" the waitress says, smacking her gum as she chews.

Dylan watches her jaw bounce, making no move to speak, so I order for us.

"Can we get two of the house-made root beers, please?" I ask.

"Sure, sweetie."

As soon as she's out of earshot, Dylan leans closer to me. "Just to clarify, you actually expect me to *eat* at this establishment?"

I laugh, but the loudness of it is drowned out by the rock music that's piped through a blown-out overhead speaker.

"You know this—" I gesture around us. "—is actually more normal than your life. Not everyone has a chef preparing fancy tiny meals and cleaning up afterward."

He nods, accepting my words without a fight, and decides he is going to try and be comfortable in this place. At least, that's what I think is behind his deep exhale and the softening of his posture.

We're both wearing our school uniforms, probably a poor decision on our part considering the amount of barbecue sauce that's about to be in our vicinity.

"Any flavor preferences?" I ask him.

"Reed," he says, putting the menu back in the holder at the edge of the table. "This is a one-time-only offer in which I'm telling you that you're in full control of how this plays out."

"Ooh," I mock. "The power is already going to my head."

He rolls his eyes.

"Do you prefer flats or drums?" I ask.

"Pardon?"

His eyes drop to my chest, and I swat at the air in front of his face.

"For the *wings*," I clarify. "Flats or drums?"

He looks at me with confusion, confirming my suspicion that he hasn't had a chicken wing in his life.

It's both disappointing and wonderful that I'm about to break him in.

When the waitress comes back, she drops our drinks and a container of peanuts in front of us. I order three different wing flavors, curious to see what Dylan's interested in, and a few sides to try out just in case he finds the entire experience too messy to indulge.

I crack a few peanuts open, breaking the shells into pieces just because I can.

"Do you enjoy this? It's so...sloppy." His nose wrinkles in disgust.

"You have no problem exchanging saliva with a number of girls in the public eye but somehow getting sauce on your fingers is offensive?"

"Different standards, I suppose."

"And what's *that* supposed to mean?" I demand.

I'm waiting for him to say something terribly offensive and cold-hearted. In the few hours we've spent together, he's been almost too nice, and I've let my mental suit of armor drop.

He pauses, watching me tap my fingers on the table before he speaks. "You know what's interesting about you, Reed? When people point out your insecurities, you face them head on. But when people challenge something that you can't immediately rationalize, you don't take it well."

"I don't know what you mean," I admit.

I've never had someone study me. Or at least, no one has ever admitted it to my face.

"For example, if I tell you that you're a control freak who is in need of a new hairstylist, you take it in stride. I'm not sure if it's because you've heard these things so many times in your life or if it's because they're insults that you understand at a basic level, but if I tell you that our standards are different, you're bound to hound me for hours until you've picked apart the argument. And the worst part is that it's not even to prove me wrong or right, it's because you genuinely want to understand why I'm saying what I am and what the basis of it is."

It's not even the words, which are completely accurate, that floor me; it's how easily they're said. Like he came to the conclusion long ago during his own psychoanalyzing of me, and that surprises me.

Dylan Archer has paid attention to me long enough to get to the root of who I am as a person and the way my mind works.

I doubt James, who I've known since birth, could articulate that.

I mull that realization over as I fish out a hair tie from my pocket. I'm still a bit too stunned to respond, so I set to work taming it into a messy ponytail on the top of my head, buying myself some time.

"You look ridiculous like that," he says once I've tamed the curls.

I roll my eyes. "Consider it payback that you have to look at it."

"Payback for what? An accurate statement about the way your mind works? I can't imagine what the payback would be if I wronged you in some way."

"Black eye. Fourth grade. Remember?"

He rolls his eyes at me, but he's all smiles with the server, who returns it as she drops off the baskets of wings, french fries, rolls, and veggie sticks for us. I try to explain the merits of both blue cheese and ranch to Dylan, but he simply pushes the ramekins of both over to my side of the table.

"No cutlery I'm assuming?" He says it with a frown, but I sense the underlying eagerness to try one of the beautifully fried and fatty wings that are coated with their famous lemon pepper seasoning.

He can deny it all he wants, but I can see his fingers itching to try one.

"Just go for it, Dylan," I encourage him.

Our conversation as we eat is limited, but he does comment on the taste of each seasoning and the way they're prepared before he picks at the sides.

I eventually persuade him to taste the fries with various dipping sauces.

I find humor in the contrast between him within this setting, hands coated in sauce, and the way he handled a knife and fork in the dining room in front of his mother.

"What do you think your parents would say if they could see you right now?" I ask him.

He pats the corners of his mouth with the napkin, just like his mother does, before he answers me. "They'd probably be too mortified to even acknowledge me as their son."

I laugh. "Probably."

"Either that or my father would drag me out of here by the neck of my shirt," he adds.

This one line confirms my suspicion about how he has been treated at home his entire life.

Roughly.

Even when my parents have been upset or angry, I've

never truly felt anything but safe and loved in my house, and it hurts somewhere deep inside me that Dylan hasn't had that same experience.

"Your dad is…"

"A total dick, yeah," he says bitterly. "I know."

The server clears off our messy table and slyly drops the check toward Dylan's side of the table.

I reach for it, but I'm not fast enough. Dylan insists on paying, dismissing my protest with one glare.

My mom texts me again. *We're going to bed!!!!!! Early meetings in the morning!! Don't stay out too late!!!*

It's already nine o'clock, which is half an hour past the curfew they set for me on school nights when I started my freshman year of high school. I guess they either forgot, don't care, or are preoccupied.

Okay. Will be home soon!

As soon as I say it, though, I realize I'm not ready to be home just yet.

Even though I'll pay for it by being tired when my alarm goes off in the morning, when Dylan and I walk to my car, I inform him that it's now time for dessert.

"More food?" Dylan says, surprised.

"Well, I guess it's not food, but it's more like sugar, chocolate, and fat reprocessed into things that are, in fact, edible."

"Do you eat like this every night?"

I laugh. "Sometimes."

I drive us five minutes down the road to a gas station that's busy even for a Thursday evening. This seems to surprise Dylan more than the crowd at the wing place.

"What could we possibly be eating here?"

"Well, it depends," I say. "What's on your Mount Rushmore of candy?"

"Mount Rushmore?" Dylan repeats as I turn off the car. "Is there something problematic and tied with slavery about candy?"

"Oh." I never considered that. "I was just asking you to name your top four candies. It's a stupid thing that James and I always say when picking our favorite things. Like 'Who's on your Mount Rushmore of singers?' and things like that."

Thankfully, he rolls right past the mention of James.

"I don't really eat candy," he admits. "I mean, I have before, of course, but I can't say I make it enough of a regular habit to put them on a national monument."

This checks out with what I know about him, so I don't make fun of him for it.

I can't remember the last time I went a day without dessert. My parents have just as big of a sweet tooth as I do, which is why we have an entire shelf of bars and bags of candy in the cabinet. We even make it a point to try all the seasonal treats in the bakery section of the grocery store.

The chocolates I had in the Archer library were so rich that it was actually a good thing they were so tiny. I probably couldn't have eaten more than two, which is practically considered a sin in my house.

Rich people's food is so boring.

"Come on, we're going to raid the store," I tell him.

Dylan has the upper hand so often that it's actually kind of wonderful to drive this entire thing forward for once.

I'm bouncing with excitement to break him in, and I

don't even think twice as I loop my arm through his as we walk up toward the entrance.

It's an innocent gesture, but it's out of habit, and Dylan knows where it's coming from.

He may have brushed past the mention of James, but my breaking the dividing line between us was not warranted, apparently. He acts like I've betrayed him, somehow, by offering him warmth and closeness.

"What are you doing?" Dylan asks, tearing his arm from my grasp.

"I don't even know," I say.

"I'm not him, you know."

"I know."

"I'm not a replacement because he's unavailable, Reed."

"Of course you're not—"

"God, it's like you can't function without the idea of him," he says sharply. "I told you, you need to get your independence, Reed, not substitute me or whoever else is around in his place. You can't even walk on your own."

He flings open the door, and I follow him, realizing that his scolding might have revealed more about his insecurities than mine.

His reaction last Friday is starting to make a lot more sense.

"What am I buying?" Dylan snaps, gesturing helplessly to the store.

I shake my head in disbelief before I grab a basket and fill it with a variety of bars and bags of sweet, savory, sour, and melty treats.

The total comes to just over twenty dollars, which is actually kind of impressive when you're only buying candy.

I slide the cash across the counter before Dylan can argue with me about another thing.

When we're back in my car, the lightness is gone, but it doesn't stop me from insisting he try every single candy bar I bought on the way home.

All things considered, I think he enjoys the experience.

And I do, too.

12

"Let's go to the movies tonight," James says.

I already planned on working more on my essay tonight. In the week since I'd started my outline at the Archer family home, I've added a few sentences to it, and I planned on knocking out a few more after James's track meet and a nice long bath.

"Come on," he says, nudging my elbow with his. "We've barely hung out all week."

That's because James is in a dating phase where he spends every single spare minute with his tongue down Lyla's throat. I'm just glad he's busy with track or else her productivity with the yearbook would dramatically decline.

This sort of behavior is standard for him. It's kind of a relief that I've never had a boyfriend or relationship that distracted me from my schoolwork in that way. I don't think I would want to be with someone who derailed me and my plans like that.

James, of course, has the benefit of copying my notes, whereas I'd be totally screwed.

"Okay," I agree.

I suppose my essay could wait until tomorrow, even though I blocked off the first half of the day to study for my Physics midterm before my parents drag me to one of their regular company outings.

Accounting seems like a terribly boring profession, but they seem to try and change the stereotype with "family friendly" outings each month. Tomorrow, we're doing a group cooking class, and they insist that I can't stay home.

"What do you want to see?" I ask.

I know that he's going to try and make me sit through a new action movie. It looks very bloody and intense.

He shrugs. "I hadn't gotten that far yet. Just wanted to make sure you're free."

It's a harmless statement, but it sits strangely with me.

A few times this week, he has texted me, asking what I'm up to with no intention of hanging out. He's checking in with me more than usual. Spending time with Dylan last week must have really thrown him for a loop, but he didn't bring it up after our text exchange.

Dylan and I have seemingly crossed the line into not quite being friends but also existing on a more personal level. I read through and gave him the thumbs up on the essay on the Billy Collins poem. He worked on a short answer assignment on the dashboard of my car after practice and yearbook earlier this week.

Now, I can practically feel the tension radiating off James beside me in Independent Study.

I got so caught up in reading last night that I didn't

realize it was midnight until I went to bed. I've been drag-ging all day, and I'm ready for the day to be over so that I can go home, change out of my uniform and binge on popcorn in a dark movie theater. Even if it's not my first choice of movie, it'll be nice to just relax and be enter-tained for a bit.

When the hours pass and I'm finally at home, rifling through the fridge for something that will soak up all the oil and butter I'm about to ingest, James texts me.

Change of plans, H. Team party at Brandon's tonight.

Brandon isn't on the team, and according to him, he doesn't regularly attend meets, so I'm curious as to how this came together. I don't dwell on it for long because I'm so relieved that I get to stay home instead.

Before you can come up with an excuse to get out of it, don't bother. You're coming with me. I'll pick you up at 7.

I groan. *James, I'm not really up for socializing tonight.*

Please, H?

I chew on my lip. I guess it wouldn't be so horrible to spend time with Brandon again. And I am kind of curious as to how everyone looks outside of their school and track uniforms.

Maybe we can just make an appearance and then I can convince James to leave early.

You owe me popcorn, I tell him.

On the bright side, I have a few hours to get ready, so I take my time doing so.

After I'm showered and dried, I pull on my fluffy robe and video call Audrey, who is also in the process of getting ready for her night out.

"I have a date tonight," she announces when the

connection goes through. "So whatever crisis of the mind you're having, it can't take up more than an hour of my time."

"And I have a party to go to," I say with a cringe.

Her eyes, slightly pixelated from the internet in her college dorm, bug out. "A party? My sister? No way."

"What do girls normally wear to parties?" I ask her.

I'm pretty sure the last time I went to an event for kids my own age, treat bags were handed out.

"Short skirt, heels, crop tops, things you wouldn't be caught dead in," she admits.

Innocent.

Cute.

Predictable.

The words James has used to describe me haunt me in that moment.

"No," I say as strongly as I can.

"No what?"

"I'm going to go to your closet, flip the camera, and you're going to pick out my outfit for me. Shoes, hair, make-up, everything."

"Is this some sort of trick?" Audrey asks.

"Nope."

She takes a long, deep breath. "Okay then."

I feel a little bit like we're kids again and playing dress-up.

She has me angle the phone so I can try on half her closet while she applies fake eyelashes, which she insists are a necessity for every night out. Unfortunately, she won't have time to walk me through the process, so I'll have to do a few extra coats of mascara instead.

By the time she's off for dinner with a hockey player and I'm waiting for James to pick me up, I feel like a total fraud.

The full-length mirror in our tiny entryway isn't forgiving, but at least it's giving me an honest reflection of her handiwork. My hair is parted in the middle and smoothed, as much as I could get it to do, in a bun at the nape of my neck.

I'm wearing large, silver hoop earrings that she got at the mall over Christmas break. I think they're too much paired with the lipstick she told me to wear, but I'm trusting her judgment on this one.

The chunky sweater actually looks cute with the high-waisted skirt, but it's a little shorter than I'm comfortable with. I dug out a pair of thick black tights from my closet and slipped on her heeled chunky boots that are actually not too terrible to walk in.

I'm second-guessing this decision when James walks in and eyes me.

"Wow," he breathes. "You look great."

I look at myself in the mirror again and frown.

It's not that I disagree with him. I think Audrey did a good enough job of micromanaging this entire look into fruition, but the problem is that I don't look like myself.

And I like being myself.

"Come on," he says, helping me shrug into my jacket. "We're already late."

James is wearing his favorite pair of dark, worn jeans and a button down I've never seen before. I wonder if Lyla helped him pick out the shirt when they were at the mall together. Usually, he's in plain T-shirts that come in a pack, but like me, he made a little extra effort for the night.

On the drive over to Brandon's house, James vents about how frustrated he is that he didn't get first in the four-hundred-meter race. Then, he flips to some of the conversations he had with his teammates after the fact.

I don't contribute anything to this. In fact, the only time I open my mouth the entire car ride is to gasp when James reaches for my hand and doesn't let go. I want to lecture him about how stupid it is to drive with one hand, even if the roads are clear and it's only fifty degrees out.

But I don't.

I stare at his warm, calloused hands and try to pinpoint the moment I started to pull away from him.

Mentally, of course.

Physically, I guess I'm destined to remain attached to him always.

A prick of discomfort hits my spine. I always say it's the little details that matter, and there's something disappointing about him owning a shirt I don't recognize and how I actively am dreading spending time with him tonight.

Things change as we get older. I know plans will shift; I've prepared for it.

Is this the beginning of the end for us?

That question has the potential to shatter me, but I pull it together when we cross the threshold of Brandon's house.

He drops my hand and hands over his car keys.

I didn't realize this was a drinking party or that James, himself, was going to partake.

Is this another thing I don't know about him? That he's a partier now?

"James," I say, grabbing his arm before he can get too far away from me. "I didn't tell my parents I would be out all night."

This is one of about one thousand reasons I don't want to stay here, including the fact that these are his team-mates, not mine, and I didn't pack a toothbrush or anything comfortable to sleep in.

"I'll drink a few now, switch to water, sleep it off, and have us back before they wake up," James says quietly and too proudly, as if he actually thought ahead to my objection and wanted to solve it. "Or you could just drive us home."

"Is this why you insisted I join you?" I ask him between clenched teeth. "So I could drive you home?"

"Of course not," he says quickly.

"James, hi," Lyla practically purrs, marching right up to step between us. "And Harper. Hey! I didn't realize you were coming."

She takes in my appearance, and her gaze isn't entirely unkind. "Cute skirt."

"Thank you," I say politely.

When they start getting all touchy feely, I make a quick exit, winding back through the large party unfolding in the foyer, complete with a DJ set up and flashing lights, to the kitchen.

Although Brandon's house is in the same neighborhood as Dylan's, it might as well be in a different zip code. It's still grand but on a much smaller scale, and there's a homey vibe here that's definitely missing from the Archer family home.

The oversized granite island in the center of the kitchen

is covered in a number of bottles and mixers, and I'm at a little bit of a loss on what to do.

There's a keg in the foyer where everyone is congregated, but I'm too intimidated to figure out how to try and work it, so I hide behind all the labels and try to figure out what's going to be the least disgusting.

The few people who pass through politely acknowledge my existence, but I'm self-conscious every time someone's gaze lingers a little too long on my appearance.

"He's not coming, you know," Brandon says.

I can count on one hand how many times Brandon and I have interacted directly, and most have happened this semester.

Even though our school isn't overly large, I don't think we've had a class together since freshman year. My only associations with him are reading his captions for yearbook, the one time we made each other less miserable at a track meet, and occasionally catching his eyes across the cafeteria when I'm trying not to look at Dylan.

"Who?" I ask innocently, keeping up our game from the last time he brought up Dylan unprompted.

I, of course, know immediately who he is referencing, but I don't bother to tell him that I was actually fidgeting over my appearance instead of fretting over the guests.

Brandon gives me a *look* with his eyebrows pulled up and lips thin.

Instead of responding, he pulls out two glasses from the shelf. I'm surprised he's using actual glass instead of the red plastic cups I've seen in movies, but I don't comment on it.

"How is tutoring going?" Brandon asks like it's a joke.

"Well enough," I tell him. "I would elaborate more, but I'm not sure if doctor-patient confidentiality also applies to schoolwork."

He chuckles and drops a few ice cubes into the glasses.

"Do your parents not care if you have parties?" I watch him pour a sizable amount of vodka into each cup. "Or drink underage?"

"What parents?" He pauses to smile at me. "The ones whose names are on the mortgage actually live in Venice or Switzerland or Vail or who knows where? Yeah, they don't give a shit."

He takes a large swig of straight vodka on ice and grimaces.

"Is having heaps of money a good substitute for parenting?" I ask.

"Mostly," he admits.

He pours a few different juices and some seltzer into the glasses, then hands me one, which I accept tentatively.

"I heard you met Andrew Archer," he says, leaning casually against the counter across from me.

Dylan's sharing stories about me with Brandon.

Interesting.

"'Met' isn't the right word," I joke. "More like 'he barked at me and seemed irritated that I wasn't Serena.'"

"Sounds about right," Brandon admits. "Andrew Archer is a complicated man. He's a prick on the outside, but once you get into his inner circle, he's..."

"Still prickly?"

"Cheers to that," Brandon says, draining half the glass in one go.

I take a few small sips. "Hey, this isn't half bad."

"Mixology is an art, love. Or maybe a science. Whatever it is, I'm the master of it."

"Is that how you got roped into having a track team party at your house?"

"Actually, I heard that Lyla and James were talking again—"

"I hate that expression," I cut him off. "Talking to someone. What the hell does that even mean? I'm *talking* to you right now, aren't I?"

He laughs but doesn't spell it out for me. "A logical argument, but the minutiae aren't important; the activities are. But, anyway, I've noticed that anywhere Lyla goes, Kyle usually follows."

"Is everyone trying to ruin the productivity of the yearbook staff this spring?" I groan and take a large sip of my drink.

"Well, Kyle and I have been *talking*, to use your favorite description, and I'm trying to progress it into a friends-with-benefits situation."

Given that we barely know each other, this is a very personal admission from him.

I assume the liquor is making his lips looser, so I'm just going to run with it.

"So, you just fool around without a defined label?" I ask him. "What do you do when you want to move on? Is there just no break up? No definitive end? How does one live without rules and parameters in their everyday—"

"Wow," he breathes. "Dylan's right. You do overanalyze to the point of exhaustion."

I bite down a grin. "Did he mention it when you two were *talking*?"

"Yes," he says, swirling the liquid around in his glass. "Your friendship is damaging his reputation."

I scoff in full confidence but shift back on my heels uncertainly. "I hardly believe that my tutoring him is hurting his reputation with Serena and all the other girls he parades around town."

He takes another drink to delay his response. I think he's wondering if he should be spilling all of this information.

Whatever emotion is splayed across my features encourages him to continue. "He hasn't been with anyone else."

I laugh. "Aside from Serena?"

"Not even Serena," he says quietly.

"Well, that you're aware of."

He shakes his head. "He's different lately. I'm still trying to figure it out, but the only change as of late is his renewed dedication to AP English and spending time with you."

I can't figure out a way to tactfully ask what Dylan has told him about our time together, so I swallow the rest of my drink.

Brandon shoves another one in my hand.

He's supposed to be Dylan's best friend. I can't believe that he would speak poorly of him to me, an associate of his enemy.

Actually, he's just telling the truth about him, but it feels like he is somehow sharing his secrets.

I compare it to my friendship with James, who would do anything for me and has told me so.

Only, now that I think about it, I highly doubt Brandon

and Dylan would make plans and then Brandon would just decide to drag Dylan to a party. I mean, he's having a party at his own house that Dylan doesn't even want to attend.

It's funny how James and I are best friends and Brandon and Dylan are best friends, and proximity plays a huge part in that. If James and Dylan grew up next door to each other, maybe they'd be best friends instead.

I giggle at that idea, earning a confused look from Brandon, who apparently dragged me into a conversation with a few of the long jumpers.

"Thank goodness you have something other than beer," one of them says.

The three girls are clearly relieved, and I can't blame them. The smell of stale liquid bread does not appeal to me at all.

"You should have Brandon make you one of these," I say, holding up my half-full glass. "It tastes like candy."

She frowns and turns to him. "How many calories are in it?"

They get into a deep discussion on macros, sugar intakes, and dieting apps, and I down the rest of my drink on principle.

I'm all for trying to improve one's health, but there's something inherently toxic about the way that stuff is marketed. Especially considering that the celebrities who push it have plastic surgeons and professional image editors at their disposal.

I try to refocus back on their conversation, but it's a little bit blurry.

I'm thirsty, so I gratefully accept another glass from Brandon. I sip on it a few times, but it doesn't quench my thirst. It somehow just makes my tongue feel like it's moving slowly in my mouth.

I go to rub my eyes and clear my vision only to recall there are layers upon layers of make-up.

"I need some air," I say to Brandon, careful not to slur my words.

"Sure you do," he says.

I don't know what that is supposed to mean.

After ensuring that the other girls are distracted with measuring out exact portions of their mixed drinks, he adds, "There's a path through the trees in the backyard. It'll take you about ten minutes to walk up to Dylan's." He stops, glancing at my shoes. "Well, maybe fifteen."

I tug on my jacket, and my feet carry me out before I can second-guess myself.

13

It's between chilly and warm outside.

Like the air couldn't decide what it wanted, so it picked both.

It might be the alcohol.

Like that guy who survived the frozen waters of the ocean after the Titanic sank because he was absolutely plastered and couldn't feel it.

Actually, that might not be a true story.

"NOT CONFIRMED!" I yell out loud.

Then I remember that I'm standing in the woods and feel stupid for saying it, but then I also recall that I'm standing in the woods and no one can hear me.

No one could find me if I stayed out here all night or if I were attacked by a bear.

Or maybe Brandon and Dylan would find me as they cross to each other's houses. Eventually. Who knows how often that actually happens.

But they probably drive now or just meet up at various

locations and talk in riddles to each other and fantasize about blowing their parents' money.

I, for one, would love to sit around and contemplate how to spend lots of money instead of worrying about things like the cost of an apartment or food in New York or how to build credit or whatever us *normal* people worry about.

That's why planning is so great.

Plans plans plans.

Everything figured out.

Always.

Cute.

Innocent.

Predictable.

I frown at those three words and shrug my jacket halfway off because I'm getting a little warm.

My toes are starting to pinch in Audrey's boots. I want to take them off, but the ground is probably frozen.

But maybe that will help the pain.

I nearly fall over when I pull them off.

When I'm almost at Dylan's front door, I power through, driving the motion forward with my arms, swinging them in exaggerated circles.

The rational part of my brain knows that although there are a number of cars in the driveway, I can't be sure if anyone's home, but Brandon encouraged me to go over.

Brandon and I are solving climate change together, so I suppose I can trust him not to send me over to collapse into Andrew or Abigail Archer's laps.

I snort, thinking about how appalled they'd be at some random teenage girl showing up drunk on their doorstep.

Is two and a half drinks enough to get a person drunk? I don't feel drunk; I just feel like my skin is alive and I'm light as a feather.

What am I doing again?

Oh, right.

Dylan.

I can't actually find the doorbell, so I squint at my phone and pull up my text conversation with Dylan.

Outside.

Your house.

I am outside your house.

Now.

The cold ground does feel nice on my feet.

At first.

I wiggle my toes to confirm I still have feeling in them.

Should I put my boots back on?

Where are my boots?

Where is Dylan?

The door opens.

I nearly squeal in excitement that it's Dylan and not either of his parents.

"Let me in, Archer," I beg, hopping from one foot to the other to avoid the ground.

Like that one time James tried to get me to play with him on the playground and told me that the mulch was lava, and we could only move if we touched the jungle gym or wood beams.

He doesn't move aside to let me in, though, because he's busy watching me bob around like an idiot. I can't help but laugh like a lunatic.

"Archer," I whine. "Please let me in. I'm cold."

"Are you...drunk?" He says it like he thinks it's funny, but I don't think I've actually been funny a day in my life.

"I think a little bit. Yes."

My honesty, at the very least, gets him to usher me inside up to his bedroom.

"I'll be right back," he says before he closes the door. "Stay here."

He leaves me standing in his *suite*.

Last time I was here, I felt like I didn't belong. I was too afraid to completely relax, but I'm pleased to find that the alcohol has removed all awareness of shame and nervousness.

I toss my jacket on the floor, which might be the most uncivilized thing someone has done in the house, and sprawl out on the couch.

Dylan returns with a few bottles of water and kicks the door closed behind him, which makes me feel like we're very alone and realize that I might actually be *very* drunk.

I drain half a bottle while lying down, and it's a miracle I don't spill a drop on myself.

I don't know how much water you have to drink before you cancel out the alcohol or how much alcohol Brandon put in my glass, but surely it adds up when combined with my empty stomach and low tolerance.

In the silence of my figuring all that out, Dylan takes me in.

"What are you wearing?" he finally asks.

I glance down and start laughing. "I don't even know."

It all seemed so chic when Audrey put it together, like I was some sort of trendy social media influencer or something, but it just seems so out of place on my body at the moment.

He sits on the coffee table and gives me another once-over. "It's not…"

"Flattering?" I prompt.

He shakes his head. "It's not you, Reed."

Dylan Archer, of all people, understands.

"Clothes are supposed to make you feel confident and more like a reflection of yourself," he continues.

"I don't think this is either of those things," I admit. "It's all my sister's doing. Her idea for making me party-ready, apparently. I thought you would be proud of me actually having something on my social calendar."

He shrugs. "Not if this is the result."

I'm used to seeing him buttoned up in his school uniform or in his track compression gear, but at home, post-familial duties, he's in black joggers and a matching hoodie.

It's a beautiful contrast with his skin and hair.

Darkness and light.

And the balance between it.

"Does this make you feel like a reflection of yourself?" I tease, which makes him roll his eyes.

I've also never seen him without shoes before. His socks are designed to look like they're decorated with little splatters of paint.

When my instinct is to reach out and touch them, I decide finishing off the rest of my water bottle is a better idea.

"Why weren't you at the party tonight?" I ask.

"My father had dinner with a few business associates. I

had to be a part of the charade while they had drinks because I'm the dutiful son and all," he explains sourly. "And I've just been enjoying an empty house ever since."

I do like to be home alone. I know it freaks some people out, but it's nice to have an entire place to yourself at your own volume and pace, deciding how to occupy a place without someone else's preferences.

I bet Dylan enjoys that same type of loneliness I do.

I roll onto my side and tuck my knees up, offering him a seat on the couch, but he stays where he is.

"Comfortable?" he asks.

I shrug. "I'm cold."

There's a walk-in closet across the room and a throw on the armchair under the window, but without hesitation, he slides off his hoodie and offers it to me.

I take it greedily. I slip it on and am very grateful that his body heat has already done some of the legwork for me.

"You're being nice to me," I comment, shimmying it down as far as it will go on my thighs.

"I'm being the same as always, Reed," he counters. "You're just not fighting every little thing I say."

I yawn and curl up again, enveloped in his warmth and scent. "Maybe you're right."

All I want to do is snuggle deeper into this couch. It's warm and smells good, and it's so peaceful here.

"Reed, someone's calling you."

"Hmm?"

I hear the vibration, but maybe it will go away if I ignore it.

"Reed, your phone," Dylan says, but this time it's with far less patience.

I begrudgingly pull my phone to my face.

It's James.

The reminder of where I am supposed to be and who I was supposed to be going home with wakes me right up.

"Hello," I say as alert and soberly as I can.

"Where are you?" His voice is a little panicked.

"I'm fine," I tell him.

He breathes a sigh of relief into his phone. "I have been looking for you all over the house. Brandon said you stepped out to get air. But you never came back."

It's not a total lie.

"Did you get a ride home?" James asks.

I turn to Dylan, who can clearly hear the entirety of our conversation. "Can I have a ride home?"

He rolls his eyes but ultimately nods.

"Yes," I tell James.

"Okay," he says.

"Have fun with Lyla." I try to say it nicely because I genuinely mean it, but there's an edginess I hadn't expected.

I hang up before he can respond.

Maybe it's because I was just talking and hearing James's voice in my ear, but the silence is loud between Dylan and me.

"Do you love him?" Dylan asks suddenly.

He says the words so quickly, as if he accidentally touched a hot pan from the oven, that I'm not sure if I've heard him correctly.

The face of indifference is placed so carefully on his features, though, so I know he's trying to withdraw any personal feelings he would have and hear the answer to the question.

"Not in the way you're implying," I say honestly. "Or the way everyone assumes."

I'm prepared for a follow-up question. He can use my lowered defenses and inebriation to get answers to whatever he's curious about, but he just nods, like I simply confirm a suspicion he held.

"You don't like Lyla then?" Dylan presses.

"She's fine," I say. "I'm just annoyed, I guess."

"At what?"

"This entire night."

"Why?"

I sigh. "Because all I wanted to do was go home and unwind from the week. Take a bath. Eat dinner. Spend an hour staring at my planner and then make amazing progress on my essay that's going to land me a freakin' awesome internship and set me on the path of actually being a successful writer instead of a poor Pittsburgh girl who has to live in her parents' basement while she fails to get anything published."

I crack open another bottle of water, needing to do something with this shaky ranting energy.

He watches me now the same way he watches me take charge in our English class. Like it's not entirely unpleasant for him to be spending his time this way.

"But no, *James* wants to go to the movies," I continue. "And then *James* wants to go to a track party. And *James* needs me to go with him so that he can promptly ditch me for someone he is *talking* to."

Dylan finally moves from the coffee table to share the

couch with me. "It sounds like you're mad at James, not the day of the week."

Normally, I brush Dylan's James-centric comments aside because they're built on years-long hatred, but this actually makes me pause. "Maybe I am."

"Being angry at your best friend is part of life, Reed," he says.

I would actually give what money I have in my checking account, all two hundred dollars of it, to watch Dylan and Brandon argue.

"I mean, not everyone can run around complimenting you all the time."

I laugh at that idea. "When have you ever complimented me?"

He rolls his eyes. "You're focusing on the wrong part of my point."

"I don't know why it's so difficult for me to admit that I am *angry* at James," I say, sitting up.

I'm too annoyed to be relaxed now, but the anger makes me feel more in control of my own body again. I guess rage makes me sober.

I tear my hair from the stupid way Audrey made me style it and run my fingers through it.

"You seem to have planned an awful lot of things around him," he says delicately. "For someone who treats you like garbage half the time then practically is attached to you the rest...it's odd that you're so loyal to him."

If I wanted to have an all-encompassing crisis of friendship and identity, I would have preferred to do it in my own room.

My head hits the back of the couch, and I groan.

177

"You know I was actually feeling really good about the essay?" I say quietly. "For the first time in months? I was actually excited to work on it tonight, but obviously that didn't happen."

Dylan stands abruptly. "About that..."

He leaves the room again, and I can't even come up with an idea of what he is doing. I just press myself into the couch while I count the seconds until he returns.

I jump when he spreads the blanket out over my legs, making me a few degrees warmer.

"Thank you." I burrow into it until I see what he has in his hands. I recognize the sleek white packaging before I even read the name on the front of the box.

"What's this?" I ask.

Of course, I'm well aware that it's a brand new MacBook Pro, the latest model that I could only dream of owning someday if I siphoned some cash from my future student loans.

I just don't know why he's holding it or why he's looking at me like that.

"I believe that you once bragged to me about the amount of words you could read in a minute, so this should be pretty obvious," Dylan says evenly, tapping the front of it.

I push back the sleeves of his hoodie to accept the box in my hands.

It's so light and beautiful, and I could weep over that alone.

"Am I dreaming?" It seems like a very real possibility.

"No, but you are coming off of a decent buzz from what I can tell."

I try to hand it back to him. "I can't accept this, Dylan. Really, it's way too much."

He rolls his eyes. "Do I really need to explain to you the proper etiquette in giving and receiving gifts? If anything, I'm doing myself a favor so I don't have to watch your hair grow three sizes in frustration every time you use your computer."

There's that self-preservation again.

Gift giving, while it seems altruistic, is actually very selfish.

You want to give to someone something to make them feel a certain way because you care about them. I see it every single birthday on my parents' faces as they watch James and me tear open the presents that they spend the other three hundred and sixty-four days tracking down for us.

Dylan won't allow me to reject this gift.

And I shouldn't deny it. I should revel in the fact that he made an effort to do something for me.

Plus, I really want it. Really, *really* want it.

"What kind of writer doesn't have a working computer, Reed?" Dylan questions, pushing me to accept the gift.

"One that still can use pen and paper just fine," I pose just for the sake of arguing.

"It's the least I can do to thank you for saving my ass this semester. I mean, it's just a computer. It won't even make a dent in my weekly allowance."

"You get an allowance?" For some reason, that's just as odd to me as Dylan actually getting me a gift.

I don't think he told me that information to brag or make me feel less adequate, but it only further confirms how different our lives are. This computer is going to be a game-changer for me and one less financial burden I have in the future, but to him, it's just another swipe of a credit card.

Dylan helps me open it. "Peeling off the film from the screen is the best part of getting any new Apple product."

I don't disagree, so I let him have the glory of it for this.

"You should have the honors," I insist. "After all, it was your money that made it possible."

"I'll accept a dedication in your first bestseller as repayment for this," Dylan says once we have unpacked it and made it through all the startup menus. "I'll probably fall asleep after that page, though, because I don't need a regurgitation of your study habits or whatever else you want to teach people about."

I shake my head. "I don't want to write those kinds of books."

"What kind do you want to write?"

At first, I think he's mocking me. I've been conditioned by James and my own preconceptions to believe that Dylan gets off on making me feel like garbage, but I'm starting to learn that it's not the case. One look at him confirms it.

"Real ones," I say. "Ones with small plot holes and unfinished sentences and characters who made bad decisions based off of their misconceptions because that's the truth."

I hover my fingers over a few letters on the keyboard.

"People read fiction because they want to escape their own reality, to jump into someone else's problems and world, but it doesn't mean you have to abandon what makes us who we are. Humans are impulsive and confusing and complex. Life isn't wrapped up in a neat little bow with declarations, it's just...yeah," I finish.

Dylan's eyes follow the motion of how I delicately trace the space bar.

"Yeah," Dylan says slowly. "It is."

I cross my arms across my chest, as if I need to hold myself together as I say the next few words.

"Whenever I read books, I never want the girl to stay with her high school boyfriend. I always want her to go off and find new adventures and new loves, but isn't there something kind of lovely about finding the love of your life early enough that you get to experience all of these things together? Like, really grow up together, challenge each other, make each other better as you face everything in life, and everything else?"

Dylan scoffs, and my defensive emotional walls are too shattered to try and repair themselves before he speaks.

"Well, I'm sure Lawson will sign up for that whenever it fits into your plan," he says with an edge.

I blink.

Because I wasn't even thinking about James.

But I wasn't talking in hypotheticals either.

And that realization is what I imagine getting punched in the face in fourth grade feels like.

Oh my god.

Dylan shifts away from me slightly to pick up the remote. I can see the frown on his face, but I can't explain what is swirling around in my mind. It's everything all at once, and I need to get it somewhere else.

I pull up a blank document and let it all spill out.

My fingers fly as I recount the years of internal pressure

I put on myself to be this good, productive human, but all it has done is suppress who I want to be creatively and as a person in general.

Trading dates on a calendar for the freedom of expression is not something that I need to be doing. Perfection isn't relatable. Being a writer or an artist is about enjoying the messy parts of life and uncovering the beauty of it.

I don't know how long I keep going because the world blurs around me as I let go of everything and keep writing.

It's like I'm flying on a different wavelength of existence.

I'm weightless, soaring above myself and feeling it all from a different perspective, yet I have a tether. It's no longer a tightrope, something I have to tread lightly on in fear of falling off the edge; it's Dylan, who falls asleep beside me with his hand pressed on top of my shin.

14

In the weeks after Brandon's party, I make subtle changes.

If my little experiment in altering my apperance to meet Audrey's standards taught me anything, it's that a big change that goes against who I am isn't going to work.

I'm a planner, after all, so I appreciate that things take time.

It felt like thousands of pounds were lifted off my shoulders when I reread, edited, and submitted my essay to the Press. Instead of spending the days after picking apart every single line I wrote even though it was too late to change, I promised myself I wouldn't look at it until I got an answer on the contest.

Then I channeled my obsession into more productive things. Like putting candy bars in Dylan's locker every day before school.

I called it payback for the new computer at first—until I looked up the price of said computer and laughed at the calculations of just how many Hershey bars I'd have to give him to cover the cost—and then, I just let it be what it was.

Fun.

Amusing.

Sweet.

Three new adjectives I try my best to get on board with these days.

It's the Friday before spring break, which is a notoriously easy day for schoolwork. But it's a little bit nerve-wracking to put a pause on all of our momentum for the yearbook, and it's made worse when Kyle approaches me.

"We have a crisis," Kyle says, panic seeping from his words. "Chrissy has mono."

I don't react quickly enough, so he flails his arms as if he needs to drive the point home.

"Our best and *only* photographer has a disease that lasts for an entire month! What is going to happen to our whole vibe of the senior year spread with candids and springtime lawn photos and black and white spreads if we don't actually have any of those photos?"

"Okay, we're not going to panic," I tell him as calmly as I can muster.

This seems illogical to him. "We're not?"

"We're going to figure it all out when we get back."

"But spring break is going to cost us an entire week!" Kyle exclaims. "We'll need to get all of the files to the publisher by May first."

Too many times I have fallen to the stress and panic, but his tentative freak out is only making me feel more calm.

"I know," I deadpan. "As the *editor-in-chief* of the freaking yearbook, I'm well aware of the deadlines."

Kyle at least looks sheepish at this.

"We'll figure something out," I promise him.

He blinks and straightens, as if he realizes that he is overreacting.

Me two months ago would have been right there with him, whipping out my planner and stressing over what we're going to do, how we can change the theme, and searching for a backup photographer.

Now, though, I'm fine. I simply pull out my planner and make a note to pick back up on this first thing when we're back in school.

Subtle changes, I remind myself, are going to bring big results.

I'm the last one to leave the school for the day, and I revel in the eerie quiet until the cleaning crew politely asks me to leave.

When I get home, I'm surprised that Audrey hasn't arrived yet. She texted me this morning to tell me when she left campus, but I suppose that doesn't mean she planned on coming directly home.

Instead, I'm greeted by my parents.

They're both sitting at the kitchen table on the same side and staring at me expectantly. Actually, no, they are beaming. I don't expect them to greet me with glares, but it's off-putting to see them like this just the same.

My mom taps the tabletop, bringing my attention to the three white envelopes on the table, each with the logo of a college I applied to. They're all the same size, a typical white rectangle, and I can't recall if that's a good thing or a bad thing.

It's funny how these three nondescript pieces of mail

hold all the possibilities of my future. They're the summation of years of planning, and the papers inside have the potential to set me on three different paths for my life.

"Open them," my dad encourages me.

And I do.

I start with the University of Pittsburgh.

My fail-safe, hometown school. The campus is right downtown, and it would be really convenient to be close to home.

It's not what I want, but I still breathe a sigh of relief when I see my acceptance.

I have an option. I have a guarantee to go somewhere, to take that next step in my life, and it's only one sheet of paper.

Next, I pick up Cornell and feel a sense of dread when my fingers touch the red logo.

It's what James wants. Without him, I never would have applied to the school.

One of the main reasons he wants to go there is because it's where his parents met, which is a bit strange, considering he doesn't actually like them all that much, and I definitely don't share that attachment.

"I got in," I say.

I try to sound enthusiastic, but I'm not sure it's convincing.

My audience of two doesn't notice either way because they're too busy gushing as they read the details for themselves.

I take advantage of their distraction and slide my nail along the edge of the envelope for Columbia.

I think I would have preferred to open these on my

own, giving myself the space to digest and figure out how to move forward.

Of course, I already know where I'm headed. It's where my heart wants to go, and it's more important than where James and my family want me to spend the next four years. I just need to figure out how to make it happen if I don't get the financial aid.

But I suppose I should see if I got accepted first.

I start reading. "It is our pleasure…"

A full grin breaks across my face. It's so large I can barely contain it. Actually, I realize, there's no reason for me to do so. I laugh at my own realization and my happiness just because I can.

Columbia.

New York City.

A writer's dream.

Rather, *this* writer's dream.

"It says financial aid and *scholarship* information will come within the next few weeks," my mom nearly screams. "Oh, Harper!"

They both engulf me in a huge hug, talking about how proud they are of me and that they know how hard I've worked. My parents are giddy with excitement. It's almost uncontrollable how happy and proud they are.

Tears are wiped when I am finally released from their grasp.

I literally have the future at my fingertips.

My hands shake because I *did it*. Me. All of my planning and hoping worked, and I'm never ever going to doubt myself again. I don't care that I have to come clean to

James and my parents because I deserve better. I know I do, and it has taken me too long to fully accept it.

"Favorite child is home!" Audrey yells as she pushes open the front door.

"Audrey, come in the kitchen now." My mom's voice is so strained from excitement that it sounds like she's in pain.

Audrey, with her emerald green hair, runs in, expecting us all to be held at gunpoint or gravely injured, but she shrieks when she sees the letters, envelopes, and reactions on our faces.

We do the entire group hug scenario all over again for a few minutes.

"Celebratory pizza, please," Audrey says.

"Are you using me as an excuse to get your favorite pizza?" I ask her.

She smiles devilishly. "Maybe."

By the time Audrey is unpacked and her first load of laundry is in the washer, our dinner arrives. I happily take a bite of my pepperoni and pineapple slice.

They're all still riding the high of my acceptance to all three schools. It's a lovely, warm feeling to have them share in my excitement, and I can only hope that whenever Dylan gets into whatever school he wants, his parents are equally as supportive.

Audrey pops the tab on her third Diet Coke as James lets himself in the side door.

I'm lucky that Audrey and I haven't really had sibling rivalry. Sure, she was annoyed at times when we were little and I followed her around, but our teenage years have mostly been drama-free. While I have fallen into many pathetic clichés, and tropes, this is not one of them.

Instead, it's Audrey and James who butt heads and pick fights with each other.

"Little Jamesy," Audrey coos, standing up to ruffle his hair.

"Dre," he says flatly. "Back already? I didn't realize that you could come and go from the Underworld as you please."

"Yeah, well, Satan's kind of busy destroying the earth and humanity at the moment, so I got a free pass."

"Oh, stop it, you two," my mom says. "James, come eat pizza. We're celebrating."

His eyes go wide at the sight of my acceptance letters before his face completely falters.

I know what this means, but my mom doesn't, so she presses on. "Harper got into all three schools!"

"And all the acceptance letters mention some kind of scholarship and grant money," Audrey brags.

"Getting paid to go to college, who would have thought?" My dad says this and glares at Audrey.

"Hey now, at least I'm going in state to a public college," she reminds them. "Not some fancy private smart people school."

The three of them laugh, but I just watch James eye the living room like he can't get away from my family fast enough, which is definitely a first for him.

"What's wrong?" I should pull him aside and ask this question, but the words fall out of my mouth before I can stop myself.

He chews on his bottom lip, then finally says, "I got waitlisted."

Audrey gasps, and the rest of the conversation halts immediately.

My parents jump into comforting mode, assuring him that it's just a roadblock that should be resolved soon enough and maybe if he wrote the university a letter or something to reiterate his interest?

I'm not surprised at how my parents are reacting, but I don't even want to think about how devastated his will be.

"Come on," I say, grabbing his hand and pulling him into the living room.

"Sucks to suck," Audrey mumbles before I turn away.

James throws himself on the couch in deep dejection.

"I'm so sorry," I say, sitting beside him. "But waitlisted isn't a bad thing. They're probably just sorting things out before they officially accept you."

He tears his fingers through his hair. "I'm just going to pretend like you're right."

"Did you hear from any of your backup schools?"

At this, his face pales.

"You did apply to other places, right?" I say cautiously.

He swallows. "I, uh, didn't get around to it," he admits.

Of course he didn't.

Because even with me dragging him along in school and reminding him of deadlines and other important details, he somehow always manages to do the bare minimum.

Even though I shouldn't, I pace around and start thinking about ways he could get around this. Maybe do some sort of late application to one of the places around here and transfer the following semester if he needed to.

I'm ready to start spitballing ideas with him, but when I try to meet his gaze, I see that he's already sucked into his phone. He's texting lazily, like he's not even fully committed to ignoring me, but it still irks me.

Normally I would be jealous or playing the part of the dutiful best friend, but I realize I don't care.

It's not that I'm not invested in James's happiness; it's the fact that I don't feel the need to obsess over him or gloss over the fact that he's being rude as hell.

"James," I snap to get his attention once more. "Did you want to talk, or did you just want me to sit here and watch you text?"

"Sorry," he mumbles, shoving his phone in his pocket.

Instead of talking to me, he stares distantly off in disappointment as I talk at him.

Eventually, I give up and send him home with a plate stacked with pizza, telling him that I'll be here for him if he needs to talk anything out or come over when he tells his parents.

As I watch him cross the space between our two houses, I realize that he didn't even congratulate me.

"Some kind of best friend," I say.

We Reeds easily slide right back into celebratory mode. Audrey being home for an entire week only sweetens everything, and even though James is acting like a royal jerk, I'm the happiest and most content I've been in a long time.

When I head up for bed, I trip over Audrey's borrowed boots. Brandon retrieved them for me after the party and dropped them on my desk in the yearbook office with a smug look on his face.

Since that night, Dylan and I have had many subtle

changes as well. We still challenge each other and work together in English, but it's almost...friendly. Like we're actual friends or something.

Friendly friends would definitely be happy for the other's accomplishments—hopefully more so than my actual best friend—so before I can stop myself, I grab my phone and fire off a text to Dylan.

I got in. To Columbia.

His response comes back almost immediately. *Do they have good chicken wings in New York?*

I laugh, pull up an article titled "The 17 Best Chicken Wing Eateries in New York City," and send it to him.

I don't know, Reed. The ambiance, stale peanuts, lack of cutlery, and allure of Western Pennsylvania will be tough to beat...but you'll make it work.

That's his form of "congratulations."

I doubt the smile on my face fades away even after I fall asleep.

15

Audrey and I spend the first few slow and lazy days of spring break almost completely horizontal.

Normally, if I sit still in one place for too long, I get itchy, like I'm allergic to downtime.

But this week, I make a point to not even take my planner out of my school bag because I want to slow down and enjoy the precious time with my sister, and it's the easiest thing in the world.

She claims the entirety of the couch for herself while I curl up in a nest of pillows and blankets on the floor.

In my next life, I'm coming back rich as hell, and I'm going to get the same exact oversized leather couch that Dylan has in his room. And whoever Audrey comes back as will have to lay on the floor in front of it.

The only bonus of this setup is that she doesn't notice the black hoodie I'm wearing is not mine or that I'm hoarding the best candy—the leftovers from the latest round I put in Dylan's locker—in the front pocket.

She's distracted by the television, sucked into some show about vampires that I do enjoy. It's the perfect blend of action, tension, and fluff, and it's one of many things she put on her "perfectly curated watch queue" for us.

I roll my eyes each time she brags about it but silently give her credit. There seems to be no end to the shows and movies, and they're all the perfect amount of drama, angst, and sweetness that I love.

When my parents arrive home from work on Tuesday night, they inform us that this behavior cannot continue. Audrey makes a huge fuss about how we're *relaxing*, not doing drugs or robbing banks. She's smug about her argument, but when my parents bang around in the kitchen and then wake us up before they leave for work on Wednesday, it's clear that it didn't work in our favor.

"You shouldn't be cooped up all day," my mom says. "It's not healthy."

"What's not healthy is making us feel bad for living our lives the way our current financial means—"

My dad sighs. "What happened to the money we sent you for food this month?"

"That's not important," Audrey presses on as my mom throws her hands up. "What is important is that I would love to take my baby sister out on field trips so we can enjoy our lives while we're still young and beautiful, but we're unable—"

My dad fishes in his wallet. "Will sixty work?"

That shuts her up. "Should be suitable. Thank you, my good sir."

Audrey holds out her hand expectantly, but he hands the cash over to me.

"I think we all know who to trust in this situation," my dad says.

"The favorite child," I say with a smile.

Audrey rolls her eyes. "Fine, but I get to pick where we eat lunch."

Lunch, as it turns out, is just us spending the entirety of our budget on various items from the food court mall.

Not that I'm complaining as I stare down an enormous plate of my favorite egg rolls. But I did see at least one book that piqued my interest in our small local shop before Audrey dragged me over to watch her try on sunglasses that we definitely could never afford.

"What's James up to?" Audrey asks me between obnoxiously loud sips of her milkshake remnants.

"I don't know," I admit.

We've texted a few times since the whole waitlist news came in, but I think he just wants to be alone—or with someone who didn't get into three colleges at once.

"What do you mean you don't know?" she demands. "You two practically share the same set of lungs."

I shrug in response. "Not lately."

"Is he still being a moody brat about how he didn't get into the *one* school he applied for? God, even my backups had backups. It's not your fault he's an idiot—"

"It's not that. Or maybe it is." I wipe my greasy fingers on a napkin and toss it onto the tray. "Things have just been different these past couple of months."

This interests her more than her slurping noises. "Different...how?"

"Spending less time together, for one."

I twist the end of my hair around my finger, marveling

at how it somehow feels smooth. Audrey begged to give me another makeover for the day. I refused outright but eventually conceded to letting her braid my hair because she insisted it would be far more manageable if we ended up trying on any clothes while we shopped.

"Well, that's just a little hiccup in your grand life plan, right?" Her tone is kind, but she's mocking me.

"Plans change," I say sharply.

"*My* sister? Changing plans? I don't think so." She laughs. "H, you started looking at different retirement account options at age ten. You've got this life all figured out and then some."

"I don't," I tell her sternly. "And it's perfectly fine."

She looks at me like she doesn't recognize the person sitting across from her.

I don't falter under her scrutiny, silently challenging her to press me further.

Eventually, she composes herself and switches the subject. "So this place has changed since the last time I was here. It's, like, all fancy now and stuff. Who do they expect to want to shop here at all these designer stores?"

She's glaring at the luxury watch store, and I turn my head to see a flash of very familiar blond hair.

I'm glad I had the wherewithal to change before we left the house because I'd be totally mortified to be seen in public wearing his clothing.

Dylan appears to be wandering around somewhat aimlessly, which I know for a fact he doesn't make a habit of doing. Deliberate might as well be his middle name.

He stops to look at one of the displays, keeping one hand in the pocket of his dark jeans while the other rakes across the top of his head. He might as well be one of the people on the posters modeling the watches, not considering buying them.

Audrey is still rambling on about the cost of a diamond watch versus rent when I pull out my phone to get Dylan's attention.

What time is it? I text.

I watch as he pulls it out, squints in confusion at my message, and then smirks.

He turns in almost a complete circle when he finally sees Audrey and me, and he doesn't hesitate to walk over even though I'm not alone.

"Are you even paying attention to me?" Audrey asks, alternating between chewing and sucking at her straw for what I hope is the final time.

"No," I admit, biting a smile as Dylan approaches.

She follows the line of my gaze. "Dylan Archer?"

"Audrey Reed," he says simply.

It's a formal greeting, and it makes me a little nervous. "You two know each other?" I ask.

He looks at my sister, waiting for her to elaborate, but she actually blushes.

"Audrey dated Brandon's older brother last summer," he fills me in. "They spent *a lot* of time in his bedroom, which is, unfortunately for us, right next to Brandon's."

"What?" I ask her, only slightly disturbed by this information. "You never told me that."

"I'm not James," she brushes me off. "I don't tell you every little thing."

"But I thought you were hung up on that guy from your Ethnic Studies class last summer?"

She shrugs. "Things change," she says, looking at me pointedly. "Apparently."

I decide that I hate my sister and her insinuations, so I pretend she doesn't exist. It's easy enough, considering she's officially given up on her milkshake and seems perfectly content to watch whatever conversation is about to unfold between Dylan and me.

We haven't talked at all since I told him I got into Columbia, but I've thought about him enough. It's hard not to when you stay inside for days, watching actors pretend to fall for each other on the screen. Eventually, you liken yourself to the characters and their situations, and then you're totally screwed.

"Are you here to buy a watch for the same cost of feeding a third world country for a year?" I ask him.

He scoffs. "A year?"

"Oh, right, I'm sure you want the one with diamonds around the face," I say, pointing to the most gaudy, and probably most expensive, one on display.

He wrinkles his nose. "Hard pass, but I'll keep it in mind for your birthday gift," he says lightly. "I'm actually here shopping for my mother's."

Audrey guffaws, and we both look at her.

"That's the line every sleazy guy uses in the movies when he's actually buying lingerie for his mistress or whatever," Audrey explains.

Dylan clears his throat. "Well, I won't be buying lingerie for my mother, but I am going to go check out a few items they held for me at Tiffany's—"

"In the backroom?"

"Yes?"

"Stop," Audrey says. "That's true? There's actually a secret room of fabulous jewels somewhere in that store?"

Dylan smirks. "I wouldn't give it that nice of a description, but yes, they have some items set aside for me to come check out."

Audrey's practically itching for an invitation, and I'm surprised that Dylan actually gives her one. "I'm actually pretty bad at picking out jewelry. If it's not too much trouble, maybe you could help me out?"

"Yes!" Audrey squeals, jumping up immediately.

Of course, leave it to Dylan to invite her along in the most convoluted way.

They carry on conversation between the two of them while I pick up the trash and toss it in the bin.

"Her birthday is tomorrow," Dylan answers a question I didn't hear Audrey ask.

They're both significantly taller than me, so I have to walk fast to keep up.

"A last-minute gift giver," Audrey says. "I like that. One time I did all of my shopping on Christmas Eve. My parents were actually super pissed because I used it as my excuse to skip out on going to church."

"Audrey, you do it every year," I deadpan.

She flips her hair over her shoulder, and I can't help but laugh.

We're so different in personality and appearance. Audrey wears a crop top, high-waist pants, and a giant, pink fuzzy zip-up, where I'm in simple jeans and a navy blue sweater. She's all pizzazz, and I'm plain as can be.

Even with Audrey's outrageous looks, Dylan gets all the attention when we step into the store.

We're ushered past the counters and led to a backroom the size of our living room. The carpet is plush and the chairs just *look* expensive, but they're nothing compared to the diamonds that one of the employees brings out from the back.

He wears white gloves and rearranges the pieces constantly while he talks about the carats and settings and everything else. The various earrings, necklaces, rings, and bracelets shimmer in the light.

"What do you think?" Dylan asks.

"The ruby earrings are pretty," Audrey comments.

I agree, but they just don't seem right for Mrs. Archer. I've barely spent time with her, but I don't think she'd ever wear something that would draw that much attention to herself in such a blatant way.

"But so is that ring."

Dylan nods at her, but he waits for me to voice my own thoughts.

He wants my opinion, apparently.

Me. The girl whose exterior he mocks regularly is required to give an opinion on jewelry that I would never be able to afford, let alone wear if I could. I barely remember to put on the lotus earrings sometimes.

I lean forward, taking another look at the display in front of us.

"The bracelet," I say with easy confidence.

The one I gesture to is no less exquisite than anything else offered, but it's understated in a perfect way. The round diamonds wrap around the entirety of the piece, but the pear-shaped ones are arranged in clusters that look like small flowers. I could visualize Mrs. Archer wearing it with a cocktail dress at her next art gallery function.

"It's perfectly elegant for her, and diamonds are her birthstone," I explain.

"I'll take it," Dylan says.

I can't even imagine how many zeros are about to be swiped on Dylan's credit card.

I find humor in the fact that he's using his parents' money to buy them gifts, but I guess that's what every parent has to deal with until a child has branched out on their own. My meager savings from babysitting last summer merely covered the cost of cupcake mix for my mom and dad.

Dylan carries around one of the famous little blue bags while we wander around the rest of the mall together.

Audrey is much more patient with me when we make our return to the bookstore. She follows Dylan around, judging all the books by their covers. I end up buying the creative writing book I eyeballed earlier, then she drags us both back to the make-up store so she can compare two kinds of mascara.

While she's talking to a sales associate, who is complimenting her skin endlessly, Dylan finally faces me head on.

"What's happening with this?" he asks, eyeing the braid that's getting looser each time I fidget with it.

I wander through the aisles. "Audrey did it to me," I say. "Said it would make things more manageable."

"Just to be clear," Dylan says. "You're taking hair advice from your sister."

Audrey's emerald green hair fades with each wash, so

it's kind of murky at the moment. I'd look like an Oompa Loompa with that color, but on Audrey, it kind of works.

I frown at his insult.

"Not that there's anything wrong with it on her, but again, I think we've established that her style is far different than yours," he clarifies.

It makes me smile with relief.

Audrey saunters back over to us with a devilish grin on her face. "I managed to get *three* testers out of that associate without buying anything," she says excitedly.

She insists that we celebrate her victory with milkshakes, even though she had one for lunch.

Dylan, of course, refuses to let either of us pay. We sit back in the cafeteria, and the conversation is surprisingly easy.

I send a silent thank you to Mrs. Archer, wherever she is, for giving Dylan the ability to hold a polite conversation with just about anyone. I'm sure hers is well practiced over years of dining with people she knows from business situations, but Dylan actually seems to be enjoying himself.

He asks Audrey a number of questions about school and what her life is like on the other side of the state. She tries to pry out of him where he's going next fall, but he expertly pivots the conversation back to her before she even realizes what is happening.

Watching him work is kind of an art.

And I'm enjoying admiring it.

After we're all sugared up and full, Dylan insists on walking us back to Audrey's car.

She pulls him into a quick hug and beelines for the driver's seat, graciously giving us a moment to ourselves.

"Thanks for the milkshakes, Archer."

"It's only fair that I repay you for all the sugar you've been gifting me these past few weeks," he says.

"Is that how it's going to be?" I ask. "Both of us trying to one-up the other and refusing to admit that it's just nice to do things for each other?"

"Maybe."

His hands are back in his pockets, and I follow his eyes across the parking lot to the spot where his lips were on mine. That night seems like years ago at this point, but as soon as I recall the memory, it seems very fresh.

I don't dwell on it too often because I think we were different people in that situation, testing the limits of each other. I wouldn't say we've figured everything out since then, but it feels evolved somehow.

But now, standing here with him, the suppression of that moment is lifted, and I can't think of anything other than how it felt when his lips were on mine.

My hand on his chest.

His lips on my neck.

The low moan in his throat.

I feel the redness creep up on my neck and cheeks. "Well, I guess I'll see you around, then?"

"Sure," he says.

There's a hollowness in his voice that makes me desperate to know if he was just thinking about the same things I was.

I chicken out from any physical contact and stutter-step over to the passenger's seat.

I'm thankful for the fact that Audrey seems to be lost in her own head while she drives because I'm floored by the flood of everything that is Dylan Archer and our kiss. And the fact that I didn't realize how much I missed seeing him every day until just now.

Abruptly, Audrey turns down the music.

"I thought you and James..." She sighs. "I thought you had a grand plan where you died sitting on a porch hand in hand after celebrating a hundred joint birthdays together."

I keep my gaze fixed out the window.

If I close my eyes, I can still see them—the life events and decisions that would lead to my death. It's like I'm taking steps along a path, focusing so strictly on getting to the end of it that I'm completely missing all the other stones I'm stepping on to get there.

For so long, I've been dwelling on an end that's so far away, along with the problems and worries that don't even exist yet, when I should have been grasping what was in front of me and enjoying the start of something special.

"I guess things really do change," she breathes before she turns the music back up.

16

"Apparently it's not even mono," Kyle groans. "But she's not coming back soon, and we're screwed."

We're two weeks back into school after spring break, and each day has been busier than the last. I miss the long days with Audrey and the mostly nothingness that filled them, but in some ways, it feels good to be back and managing my schedule and schoolwork.

There are some loose ends that need to be tied up, and a major one is putting the final touches on the yearbook before we send it off.

It's just Kyle and me left for the day. We're both huddled over my laptop and making a list of pages that need correcting and spaces we need photos.

I pinch the bridge of my nose. "Let me ask the front office if we can have some budget to bring in a professional."

"You think it's worth all the hoops of getting written

permission and having them vet people to roam the halls and shoot candids?"

"Why don't you just have students send in their own photos?" Brandon says from the doorway. "We all have thousands of pictures and selfies on our phone. Why not take advantage of it?"

I watch him pull up a chair and kick his feet up on the tabletop, like some sort of CEO who just sauntered in to solve all our problems.

To be fair, he kind of just did.

"That's actually genius, Brandon," I say.

"More than just a pretty face with a multimillionaire best friend," he says with a smirk.

I roll my eyes. "Okay, let's talk logistics."

Kyle sets up an email address for submissions and then together we draft a note for the front office to distribute to teachers and to the student body. Brandon suggests we make flyers as a reminder, and we make good progress on those until he interrupts us, reminding Kyle they have dinner reservations.

I finish up the flyer without him, and I check my email once more for good measure before I shut down for the night. It's mostly junk and messages from the PTA, but occasionally I'll get something from the dean or one of the school board members.

"Oh my god," I say, nearly falling out of my chair when I see the unread message in my inbox.

My heart pounds as I click the message and digest the words inside it.

Dylan knocks on the door with his knuckle. "Hey, Brandon said you were still...what's wrong?"

"I got it," I breathe. "The contest, the internship, the recognition. I got it."

I turn my computer to show him the email from The Pittsburgh Press.

His eyes flicker over it briefly, confirming what I'm telling him.

"Of course you did," Dylan says like it is the most obvious thing in the world.

I think I'm in shock.

Good thing I'm sitting down.

He flips the just-washed strands of wet hair off his forehead. "Seems like something worth celebrating," Dylan says.

I blink. "Yeah, I suppose it is."

When I won the spelling bee in fifth grade, my parents took me out to a local ice cream shop and let me order the biggest size cone and whatever flavor I wanted.

That was, apparently, child's play.

Because Dylan invites me to his house, and I arrive after stopping at my parents' office to tell them the news in person, then he gives me the very fancy bottle of champagne.

"I don't know how to open it," I admit, tracing the label with my fingertips.

We're sitting side by side on surprisingly comfortable wooden chairs at the edge of his property, and although we're out in the open, it feels very private surrounded by trees and the other landscaping.

"But it's pretty," I add. "Maybe I should just keep it like this and let it sit on my nightstand."

He rolls his eyes. "Only you would use a three-hundred-dollar bottle of champagne as a paperweight."

"This was three hundred dollars?" I gasp. "Well, I definitely can't drink it now. It's like the most expensive thing I own."

"Your computer," he reminds me.

"Right," I say. "You know, you don't have to keep buying me stuff. I tolerate you well enough without benefitting from your limitless credit card."

"Why do you think it's so much fun to buy things for you?" Dylan poses. "Serena practically held her hand out on a weekly basis and was floored that I *only* got her sapphire earrings for her birthday."

He's comparing me to Serena, and the realization makes me squirm.

My mental catalog of Dylan Archer memories confirms that he once clearly referred to her as his *girlfriend*—not just someone he was *talking* to—in our sophomore Chemistry class.

I place the champagne in my bag for safe keeping, and as I'm rooting around, I pull out a Hershey bar that's long been forgotten but perfectly intact. I gently set down my bag at my feet and tear open the wrapper with my teeth.

"Classy," Dylan says, but there's no venom in it.

How long has it been since there was the classic maliciousness to his tone with me? I can't remember now.

I take a massive bite, touching a number of the little rectangles that are carved on the surface.

"I never understood the phrase 'eating your feelings' until now, Reed," he says. "But if that's how you want to celebrate, who am I to judge?"

I offer it to him, teeth marks and all. It's a terrible offering, but it's all I've got. Frizzy hair and half-eaten candy.

He breaks off a small rectangle to pop in his mouth. "I think I finalized what my Mount Rushmore is," he says once he chews and swallows it.

"I'm glad all of those early mornings of filling your locker finally paid off," I say. "What's the lineup?"

He cracks his fingers in anticipation. "For starters, the far left of the monument, Almond Joy. At first, I thought the almond and coconut combination was gross, but then it grew on me. And next, definitely a Heath bar...what? Why are you laughing? I thought you'd be ecstatic that you're going to have such a massive impact on my dental bills from all the sugar."

"It's just that you picked all of the old people's candy," I explain to him.

"And from your vast experience of socializing with the elderly, you're clearly the expert on this."

"You're funny, Archer, you know that? I'm just saying, though, those candy bars are the kind that Audrey and I tried to pawn off on each other when sorting our Halloween candy as kids."

His gaze drops to his hands, and I consider the very real possibility that he never went trick-or-treating or wore a costume in his entire life.

"And what do you think I should add to it?"

"Well, most people our age like Skittles and Sour Patch Kids and Reese's."

"My palate is too refined for those," he tells me. "Obviously."

I roll my eyes.

"I'm certainly not putting this plain chocolate on my monument," he says as he helps himself to another piece. "What else do you have in that bag of yours?"

I take the last bite and crinkle up the wrapper in my hand, then I start digging through my bag, shuffling around my books, planner, and all the other miscellaneous items that live inside.

He grabs my personal copy of *Brave New World* when I bring it to the surface and starts flipping through it. "Why do you still have this? We finished this unit weeks ago."

"I liked it when I read it originally a few years ago, but now it's one of my favorites."

"Now? Helping me with my homework stirred up a love of dystopian literature within you?"

I shrug. "There's a lot of good takeaways from that book."

"Like what?"

I stop digging through my bag so that I can level with him. "You should know. You did a ton of work for class on it."

"I do know, but I'm curious as to what yours are."

"The message that we are each individually responsible for our own happiness, and it's absurd to put someone else in charge stands out," I admit quietly.

He relaxes into the hard back of his chair and opens to one of the highlighted sections in the book. "I would have thought you were one of those people who considers books sacred, but you've pretty much vandalized this."

"I just like to mark what resonates with me in the moment," I explain. "It makes it easier to come back to that way."

I pull my feet up onto the seat and settle in, watching him thumb through the book.

It's kind of like when Audrey, knowing I would love certain scenes in one of the movies she picked, watched me for my reaction instead of paying attention to the screen.

Seeing the world through Dylan Archer's eyes was something I would have never planned to experience. Out of all the life events and possibilities I thought would happen, this wasn't even a fraction of an idea in the back of my mind.

I was supposed to help him get a good grade this year, to move on with his life, but instead, I think he helped me unwind and find a better part of myself. I don't even know if it was intentional or if that's just what happens when you're a bystander in his presence—you have to kick your legs forward or you'll never keep up with how he moves.

He thumbs through it before he stops to read one of the earmarked lines: *"Words can be like X-rays if you use them properly—they'll go through anything. You read and you're pierced."*

The timbre of his voice saying those words is almost too good.

I exhale. "Keep going," I say quietly.

When he looks at me curiously, I add, "Please?"

"But I don't want comfort. I want God, I want poetry, I want real danger, I want freedom, I want goodness. I want sin."

The look on his face is nearly indescribable, but I somehow recognize it in myself.

He's feeling the emotion of those words because they reflect something hidden away inside him that's too personal to bring to the surface through his own voice.

It's what good writing does to you.

But it's not just that. I'm well aware of those words in the context of Dylan and me.

The sun is just now getting around to setting, creating a mid-spring orange hue. The sky's so far away, but somehow it surrounds us. It's too early for the summer bugs or flowers to bloom, which means it's just us out here, claiming the wet green grass and crisp air for ourselves.

Dylan's fingers trace the words before he says them, but finally, he whispers, *"I want to know what passion is. I want to feel something strongly."*

I watch the words come out of his mouth and the way he swallows after he finishes.

He slowly closes the book and drops it back into my bag, as if he needs to distance himself from those revelations that he brought between us.

"Harper," he sighs, as if that word is actually a little painful to vocalize.

He closes the distance between us, pulling me to my feet and crushing me to his chest before I can tease him for saying my first name.

His eyes are wild, like he's not totally in control of his reaction at the moment but he so desperately wants to give in.

With shaky fingers, I touch his chest, then his neck, and finally, his cheek. I caress the line of his cheekbone, then his jaw. Just like I did last time, but now, there's something even deeper in the movement. I'm not proving a point; I'm memorizing him.

I stand on my tiptoes, trying to reach him, but I fall short.

He closes his eyes briefly, and when he opens them again, I see the same look on his face as I do when he's on the track.

It's the stillness before the start.

The one final breath before the jump.

The serenity before the chaos.

But he's not about to burst off the starting block. He's in my arms, and he's on the brink of something that's going to require much more of him than any sprint would.

The silence is loud, but his decision is clear.

His lips meet mine.

I'm expecting the dominant version of him, the one that crushed his lips against mine to prove a point, but he's careful. He's using his mouth to ask permission to break down whatever barrier still exists between us.

Dylan's hands move from my hips up to wind in my hair. I put my hands on his wrists, holding him to me as his tongue parts my lips.

It should be terrifying to open myself up to him, to give into the feelings between us and what that means, but it's effortless.

I no longer acknowledge the passing of time or the complications this is going to cause in my life plan because I'm just going to give in to him and the faint taste of chocolate on his lips.

17

I give myself permission to revel in the newness.

As humans, we experience it all the time on our own, but for me, the new experiences of being with Dylan Archer are all-consuming. Every single moment with him feels like something I shouldn't be indulging in, but I can't help myself.

The kisses in the stairwells between classes are brief but fiery.

The way Dylan runs his fingers over my palms and wrists while he drives is divine.

The looks I get across the cafeteria are equal parts promising and irritating.

It takes me ten days after our first real kiss to resurface.

"Where are you, H?" James says, waving his hand in front of my face.

I blink to see that James and my parents are staring me down like they're waiting for me to faint or explode or do something other than pick at my dinner.

"What?" I ask, touching my face to make sure there's no drool or blood or something on it.

"You just willingly let me have the best piece of garlic bread," James says, taking a massive bite of the perfectly done middle bite.

Thinking about kissing Dylan Archer is actually better than crispy brown crust, warm center, and gooey cheese topped with garlic and basil.

Of course, I don't say that out loud.

"Sorry," I say lamely. "I'm just lost in thought."

This dinner is supposed to be a celebration of my winning the writing contest. My parents insisted on doing something to recognize my achievements, but somehow instead of going out to the restaurant of my choice, we ended up at home eating James's favorite meal.

Not that I'm complaining—it was nice of them to be proud of me, but it wasn't my first or second choice of ways to commemorate a success. For college, I had to eat Audrey's pizza, and for the internship, it's James's lasagna.

Plus, James and I hardly spend any time together these days. He's gearing up for the big invitational that marks the end of the season and his high school track career, and I'm busy with my school work, yearbook duties, and Dylan Archer.

In theory, it was nice to be around him, but in practice, I would have rather had a quick meal with my parents, then headed up to my room to stare at the final yearbook proofs that we're sending to the printer tomorrow.

"So, I have good news," James says, reigniting the stalled conversation.

"Oh?" I say before I shove a big bite in my mouth,

deciding I'm going to actively participate in moving this meal forward to its end.

"Cornell officially accepted me! I just found out this afternoon."

"That's great," I say, and I try to mean it.

We all offer him congratulations and hugs around the dinner table.

It's not hard to fake my enthusiasm for him.

I know how much it means to him to go to the same school his dad did, even if he's usually at odds with his parents. There's practically a sweatshirt with fraternity letters waiting for him the moment he shows up to campus, a place he loved from the first minute we toured it.

My parents ask him all sorts of questions about declaring a major and trying out for the track team through the rest of dinner, sparing my contribution from the conversation.

After slices of chocolate cake, now dug into with dual purposes of celebrating, and a final round of congratulatory hugs and pats on the back, James heads home.

I'm up to my elbows in bubbles at the sink, scrubbing the dishes that are too big to go into the dishwasher.

My dad turns on the television in the other room, trying to catch the end of some baseball game, and my mom takes his usual spot beside me to dry after I wash.

"I was thinking tomorrow we could go to that store where Audrey got her dress? And then get lunch after? Make a little girl's day out of it."

"What?" I ask, snapping to attention.

"For prom," she clarifies. "James was dropping hints throughout dinner while you were being a space cadet."

"He's dating Lyla, Mom," I say automatically. "Or *talking* to her. Or whatever."

"Still wouldn't hurt to go at least look at dresses and maybe try a few on." She shrugs and towel dries one of the pans. "You can always ask the boy who took you to Homecoming."

It's not like my mom to use suggestive sentences like that.

She's usually very direct in what she wants from me, especially when it's about how she wants to spend her weekends, the precious time set aside to not worry about work. My planning gene did come from somewhere, after all.

Still, I'm not buying the air of innocence she has on this topic. It's confirmed when I notice that she's biting back a smile.

"Mom," I say.

She reaches in the sink to pull the plug.

"Mom," I repeat.

When she ignores me again, I flick the water from my hand at her, making her laugh and hold up the towel in defense.

"What did Audrey tell you?" I demand.

"Your sister? What does she have to do with this? I just have the feeling you're going to have a date, and we want to be prepared, don't we?"

I groan and head upstairs to call Audrey, but she sends me right to voicemail.

My mom keeps up the ruse of innocence through the

next day, occasionally asking me who I'm texting as we drive on the highway. Sadly, it's only Audrey.

Dylan is spending the day at some yacht club—because apparently those aren't things that only exist in movies—with some of his father's business associates and would earn some glares if he was on his phone the entire time.

"What is your sister up to today?"

"Being really hungover and mad that we're going shopping before noon," I tell her before I can stop myself.

"Tell her to get a mimosa and get over it," my mom says.

I feel my eyes widen in my skull. "Since when did you get so laissez-faire about underage drinking?" I ask her.

"She's in college, and it's the weekend. I know how these things go."

I sputter for a response.

"It's not like we didn't have cheap beer when I was in school."

"Mom!" I say.

"What else do you think you're going to do during winters in Ithaca? I know you can read until your brain gives out, but I'm sure James will do an adequate job of getting you to at least one party before Thanksgiving. And don't think I haven't noticed that bottle of champagne in your room..."

She laughs as she finds us a space near the entrance to the dress store. It's a monstrosity, like a full-size department store but just filled with prom dresses and other special occasion wear according to the sign out front.

Apparently this is the best store within an hour drive of our house because they make you provide your name and school at checkout to ensure that no one will show up in the same dress. It's kind of genius given their clientele.

My mom turns off the car and reaches to grab her purse from the backseat but stops when she sees the expression on my face.

She eyes me, curious as to what is going on in my head. "You okay?"

I should have told them all—my mom, my dad, my sister—all at once. Just declared what school I wanted to pick when they were in celebration mode instead of dragging it out. I was resolved to not care about their opinions and go for what I want, but as I'm about to do it, I'm nervous about disappointing them.

"What if that's not what I want?" I can barely get the words out.

"I'm only joking, sweetheart," she says delicately. "You don't have to do anything you don't want to do."

I shake my head. "What if I don't want to go to Cornell?" I ask.

This one little question opens the floodgate to all the things I have been holding in for months.

Dylan still is the only person I've told about Columbia —well, aside from the older couple from Books & Beans. But if I had known how things would turn out between us, I'm not sure I would have told him.

I thought that I could be honest with someone I'd never see after graduation. That my hidden truth would come out, and that memory would disappear from his mind along with everything else about me.

But instead, it turned into a tangible thing. Not just

Dylan, but the realization that the future I once planned for myself was not the one I wanted.

For so many years, I clung to James like a life raft. I made his wants my wants because it was convenient and easy, not because it was my choice. My parents enabled this behavior, whether they knew or not, and now, I wanted to escape from that.

I just had to get through the hard part, which was actually making it happen.

"What if I don't want to go to college with James?" I ask. "Or date him? Or end up together? Or stay in Pittsburgh or do anything that I once told you I wanted to do?"

She sits back against the seat, angling herself so she can speak to me head on.

I hold my hands together, squeezing my fingers tightly to brace for whatever she's going to say to voice her disappointment, but she surprises me when she reaches over and gently brushes my hair behind my ears.

I honestly hate when she does this. It makes my head look like a weird puffy jack-o'-lantern, but I'm so relieved that she's comforting me instead of making me sob with guilt that I almost cry in relief.

"Your father and I just want what's best for you, Harper."

"I know," I say because I've heard it one thousand times. "But don't you think going to Cornell and dating James is what's best for me?"

She laughs. "Not if you don't."

I frown. "That's not an answer."

"I don't want to tell you what to do because it's your life. As much as I love being a mom and being a part of it, soon you're turning eighteen and are going to be making all sorts of life decisions. Of course, I'm here to help you whenever you need me. But you've gotten more scholarships to all three schools than we could have hoped for, so everything is taken care of except for your decision to pick what you want to do."

It's logic.

But it's still not an answer.

Just as I'm about to tell her that, she adds, "But did I really think my little obsessive planner applied to the best writing school in the middle of New York City for no reason?"

I can't help but offer her my biggest, genuine smile.

"Now, let's go find the dress of your dreams," she says, squeezing my hand a final time. "Only the best for my favorite child."

I can't help but squeal at her admission.

And again when we finally find *the dress*.

18

"You've got this, Kyle?" I ask.

If there's anything that shows how much I've changed recently, it's that question I just asked.

We just jammed the entire yearbook staff in the office to celebrate that we've finally pulled everything together and are ready to ship it out to the printer. But now it's back to our normal skeleton crew for the official file transfer.

And I'm letting Kyle have the glory of pressing "enter" on the computer.

When he does, we're all smiles and high fives, a simple act given the months and hours we poured into this.

I even give Brandon a hug, who, in addition to writing a number of captions, has decided to give himself an honorary title of Yearbook Savior. His genius idea of student-submitted pictures did totally transform a number of pages in the yearbook.

"We should head out if we want to catch the four

hundred," Brandon says, double-checking the time on his phone.

I'm eager to get out of the windowless room and into the May sunshine, even if it's just to go sit in the stands for the big invitational. A typical meet is just two or three teams facing off, but an invitational brings in the top performers from each event in the district.

It's a pretty big deal that out of all the schools in the district, ours got to host the final one of the year.

"You coming with us, Lyla?" I ask as I gather up my belongings to join Kyle and Brandon.

I planned on standing near the fence by the finish line to avoid greeting and getting roped into sitting between Dylan's mother and James's parents, but I'm not opposed to the idea of sitting with a group of people my own age.

She gives me one of those sneers that masquerades as a smile. "I'll pass," she says in a clipped tone before she brushes past me.

I look to Kyle and Brandon for an explanation, but they're both just as confused as I am by her attitude.

"Don't look at me," Kyle deflects.

"You're her twin," Brandon says as we start to walk outside. "Don't you have a decoder ring for her behavior?"

He rolls his eyes. "All I know is that I try to avoid getting that look whenever possible."

"Well, it's not like I did anything to deserve it," I say.

"Maybe that had something to do with her and James arguing in English this morning," Brandon speculates.

"Why does that have anything to do with me?" I ask him.

Kyle rolls his eyes. "Do you really need me to unpack

the emotional availability of James and whatever weird attachment you two have to each other?"

I consider it. "No," I decide.

Brandon laughs and throws an arm over both of our shoulders, holding us together as we find seats in the semi-crowded stands.

Normally, I'm glued to the outcome of the races, mentally willing the runners forward, but today, I'm content just to watch it happen.

Brandon is right there with me, even offering funny commentary on how some of the jumpers are moving and cringing at how javelin throwing is an actual event despite it being dangerous as hell.

James's coach pulled him into a relay today, which we missed while we were huddled in the yearbook room, so the four-hundred-meter race is the first and last one he's up against Dylan for the day.

Because their qualifying times were nearly identical, they're placed side by side in lanes three and four. I can feel the tension all the way up in my seat.

They're both doing their pre-run routines, focusing on their final stretches and preparations before they're up.

After the first two heats ahead of them start and end in rapid succession, they're able to adjust their starting blocks and get in position.

The white lines on the dark red track feel narrower than they usually do.

They're freshly painted, and adhere to regulation, but with Dylan and James side by side, it feels too small to contain them. They keep clipping each other with their elbows while they stretch. James has to stand awkwardly in waiting while Dylan kneels down to slide the metal starting blocks back to where he wants them.

I'm on edge just watching them interact so closely.

The referee calls for them to get in position, and before Dylan crouches down, he looks up at me and winks.

I smile and wave in return, and James looks up just in time to see it. The line of his jaw clenches as he fixes his gaze toward the finish line.

"This will go over well," Brandon says beside me.

"Runners on your mark," the referee calls. "Get set."

He pulls the trigger on the starting gun, and they're off.

Their arms thrash until they get in their stride, but once James and Dylan pull ahead slightly from the other runners, it seems like their upper bodies are completely disconnected from their legs. They move so fast that their feet blur in my vision.

The crowd noise is impressive, but the sound of my heart beating in my ears overpowers it.

I stare at Dylan's chest, watching it heave and inch forward a fraction faster than James's. I force myself not to blink so I can watch him cross the finish line a step ahead of everyone else.

They all jog another fifty meters or so, a result of the motion and time it takes them to ease slowly to a stop.

The rest of the team dashes over to surround both of them as the announcer says that Dylan just set a district record for his finish time.

Serena throws her arms around Dylan's neck, and he awkwardly pats her on the back until she lets go of him.

While he accepts congratulations from the coach, James stomps up to him, irritation clear in his expression.

226

I sigh, knowing that James is going to be inconsolable for a while after this.

Brandon elbows me. "Oh," he breathes.

I look down at the track again, expecting everyone to be moving ahead to the next event, but a crowd of teammates and other runners are forming around Dylan and James.

Dylan stands rigid with his arms crossed on his chest. James's face is about an inch away from his. I can't tell what he's saying, but I can see the anger in his words.

Brandon and I both move on instinct, running down the stairs and weaving around people to get onto the track. Kyle is yelling behind us to wait for him, but we don't listen; we're trying to stop a car accident before it starts.

Finally, we get within earshot of their conversation.

"Are those spikes even the right length? Did you switch them after they got checked by the ref?"

"Are you accusing me of cheating, Lawson?" Dylan deadpans.

"Maybe."

"Don't you have anything better to do with your time than try and make excuses?"

"What's going on?" I ask, forcing myself between them.

"Lawson was just about to get the hell away from me," Dylan says, not breaking their eye contact while he answers my question.

It's irritating that they're both so much taller than me. Standing between them, not reaching their eye level, has done nothing to break whatever this is up.

Over the loudspeaker, the announcer makes a joke about the hometown team holding up the next race.

227

"Dylan," I say, but he still doesn't withdraw from the standoff with James.

I put my hand on his chest, one of my favorite places in the entire world to feel, which finally draws his attention to me.

Dylan and I, and our newness, haven't dared to touch each other in public, let alone surrounded by an audience and stands full of parents and classmates. He exhales and reaches up, holding my hand in his.

I smile at him, just slightly, and he returns it. I've successfully forced his hand into bomb defusal. He nods at me and starts to back us away from James.

"What the hell is this?" James demands. "Harper?"

I close my eyes, not really wanting to do this in front of the crowd, and let Dylan lead me away.

I trip when a force stomps on the back of my shoe, sending me forward into Dylan's back. He turns and catches me, righting me with a hand at my waist.

His cool mask is murderous. "What is your problem?" Dylan asks James.

It's the summation of years of anger and rivalry between them, and I'm stuck. Literally, I'm trapped staring at Dylan's chest when James pushes on the outer edges of his shoulders.

"Hey!" I try to break out between them, but they're starting to officially fight now.

I'm trying to push them apart, but they're amped up on adrenaline and testosterone, and I'm just a casualty at this point.

The coaches try to get through the circle, but the

teenage athletes are forming a blockade, eager to see how this plays out.

I once again place my hand on Dylan's chest, trying to get him to stop, but this time, it doesn't work.

I shove my other hand upward to try and stop James. The heel of my palm hits something hard, and I hear him cry out.

I turn and gasp. Dylan's rage turns into laughter at the sight of James wincing and holding a hand over the left side of his face.

"Oh my god, James, I'm so sorry," I say. "I didn't mean to."

He holds a hand up, willing me to stop talking.

"This is what it feels like to be on the opposite side of one of Reed's black eyes?" Dylan says smugly. "Not bad."

That, of course, reignites James, and they start their shoving match all over again. I'm able to dodge it as best I can until the coaches make it to us and pull them apart.

The athletic director, who I recognize from the few times he's had to give out awards during assemblies and speeches after meets, is completely red faced when he reaches us.

"You three," he nearly sputters. "In my office. Now."

"Me?" I ask, somewhat dumbfounded. "I was in the stands. I had nothing to do with this."

That, apparently, doesn't matter.

I'm silently seething as James and I sit in uncomfortable metal folding chairs outside the director's office.

Like we're in some sort of bad cop movie, he's pulling us in one at a time to give statements of what happened. He was nice enough to provide James with an ice pack before barking at Dylan to get inside his office, leaving James and me to sit in silence.

"You lied to me, Harper," James says finally. "You said nothing is going on between you two."

I roll my eyes. "You asked me that question months ago, James. And it's not like we've been having sleepovers every weekend since, staying up, brushing our hair, and talking about our crushes."

I expect him to fire back at me, but he is speechless.

"What has he done to you?" James asks quietly.

"What does that even mean?"

I know exactly what he means, actually.

The Harper he knows was timid, lost in cycles of planning and worrying, and never really doing anything of note. Too scared to go after what she wants or do anything other than follow him around like a lost puppy.

"It means...I don't know," he falters. "Things are just different between us lately."

"You're just now noticing that?" I ask.

My words are harsh, but internally, I'm cracking just a bit.

I don't want to be against him. Despite everything, I do want and need him in my life, but we need to evolve to different terms.

I can no longer be his reliable sidekick that fills a gap between girlfriends, the person whose hand he reaches for when he's feeling lonely, the doormat to his brooding.

I need a best friend who will cheer me on, just like I've done for him for so many years, and I need him to understand it.

"I'm sorry," I start before I stop myself. "Actually, wait, I take that back. I don't know why I'm apologizing."

James gestures to the ice pack that's covering the red bump forming on his cheek. "Maybe for this?"

I can't help but smile. "Sure," I say.

The sound of heels clacking down the hall draws both of our attention.

Somehow, I'm not surprised that the sound belongs to Mrs. Archer, who is dressed exceptionally well, considering she's at a high school sporting event.

She takes in James and me for a beat.

"Harper," she says evenly. "Lovely to see you again."

"You too, Mrs. Archer."

"Is my son in there, by any chance?"

"Yes," I tell her. "It's been a few minutes actually."

"Thank you," she says before knocking and letting herself in.

"So," James says and then clears his throat. "Are you and him, like, official?"

I pause as I realize we're in that undefined *talking* stage.

Well, talking and kissing if I'm being specific.

"I...don't know," I admit quietly.

James lowers his ice pack and faces me. "Look, I don't know the details, and frankly, I'm not sure that I could stomach them."

That's completely fair.

"And I know it's weird timing, but I've been thinking about this since lasagna night and..." He trails off, leaving me frozen in uncertainty at what he's going to say next. "I just was really hoping you'd want to go to prom with me."

I open and close my mouth a few times. "Won't Lyla have something to say about that?"

He looks at me sheepishly before he answers. "She dumped me this morning."

I laugh. Of course. I'm his guaranteed backup.

He reaches for my hand, and I don't immediately pull away. This is him feeling guilty but also wanting me to listen to what he has to say.

"Lyla and I...and me and the other girls...it just doesn't work. It has never worked, H, and I think I've finally figured out why."

I swallow. It's loud. I turn my head away from him, and James squeezes my hand tighter, trying to pull me back to him.

Of course, it's at that moment Dylan opens the door.

I yank my hand out of James's, but before I can open my mouth to explain, Dylan sneers, "Isn't this cozy?"

He drops in the seat next to me and makes no move to reach for my hand or take advantage of our close proximity.

"Don't let me interrupt whatever this is," Dylan says, gesturing between us.

"Dylan," I start. "It's not anything."

"What's it to you, Archer?" James seethes.

"It's just such a shame that shiner's going to mess up your face for the pictures," Dylan says. "Prom? Sounds terrible, but I'm sure you'll enjoy it."

I groan. "I didn't agree to anything yet," I tell him.

"Yet," James says.

"Well, don't let me stop you, Reed," Dylan suggests. "You're finally getting everything you wanted."

He's doing his self-preservation thing. I recognize this

and want to tell him to cool it, but I don't dare do so in front of James because it would only make the entire situation worse

I see the hollowness in his eyes, and I hate it. When I reach for him, trying to fix it, he pulls back.

Voices carry down the hall, the same one that Mrs. Archer came from, and James and I lock eyes, recognizing the sounds of both sets of voices.

James curses under his breath.

Our parents have arrived, and they're not happy. My parents aren't mad, though—they're just *disappointed.* And surprised, my dad admits to me quietly before they're ushered into the director's office. We're shut out for the time being.

"Did I hear them mention us possibly getting a suspension?" I say with a frown.

"Probably just in-school," James says. "Nothing too harsh."

"*Just* in-school suspension?" I repeat. "I didn't even do anything."

Dylan sighs. "Get over it, Reed. I highly doubt Columbia gives a crap about this kind of stuff."

"Cornell," James corrects him. "We're going to Cornell."

Dylan, once again, looks at me with his shiny brown eyes that are lifeless at the moment. "You didn't tell him?"

I pinch the skin at the bridge of my nose.

"For someone so smart, you're so stupid sometimes, Reed."

He's said those words to me before, but this time, I don't disagree.

233

19

My parents ground me for the weekend for good measure.

"No phone and no friends," my dad says.

I feel like many people would be devastated by that, but apart from not getting to clarify things with Dylan, it's a normal weekend for me that's spent reading and planning.

By Sunday night, Audrey has worn my parents down enough to video chat one of their phones. We prop her up on the table, and she insists on hearing all the details of James's black eye. She, of course, cackles in enjoyment at his expense.

I don't know if being suspended means I'm excused from classwork, so I make it a point to get to school a little early on Monday to turn in all my assignments.

Miss Delway isn't in her classroom, and just as I resign to email her or try to come back at lunch, I bump into her in the hallway.

"Excuse me, Harper," she says, delicately holding her uncapped travel cup of coffee so it doesn't spill.

"Oh, Miss Delway, I actually have today's assignment for you," I tell her, pulling it out of my bag.

She offers me a tense smile when I hand it over.

"And it's right at the word count," I add.

That softens her a little bit. "I received an email over the weekend about you and Mr. Archer both not being in today's class, so I appreciate your diligence in getting this assignment turned in beforehand."

"Of course," I say politely. "I'm not sure if he has completed this one yet, but I think he has caught up on all the makeup work as of last week, so this shouldn't be too delayed."

Her eyebrows pull together. "Makeup assignments? I'm not sure what you mean."

I stop fidgeting with the strap of my bag to make sure she's not messing with me.

I'm not on the closest terms with her. In fact, I'm far from her favorite student, much to my dismay, but she doesn't have a reason to lie to me about this, so I push back.

"The makeup work Dylan had from missing a bunch of assignments earlier in the semester?" I'm fishing, but I can already tell from the look of impatience on her face that she has no idea what I'm talking about.

"Dylan Archer? Miss assignments?" She wrinkles her nose. "It's not entirely appropriate for me to discuss other students' grades, but I can say that he is one of the few students whose grades even comes close to yours. He might not be as dedicated as you are, but I can't recall a time he has ever missed an assignment."

I blink. "Right, I must have gotten something mixed

THE STILLNESS BEFORE THE START

up," I lie. "But thank you for accepting this. I'll see you in class tomorrow."

As I walk to the tiny, windowless room near the front office that's set aside for suspensions, I come to terms with the fact that Dylan Archer lied to me.

He came to me months ago under the pretense of needing my help when he didn't, and I want to know why.

I have a sneaking suspicion that it's some nefarious reason like I suspected originally. He hated James so much he thought it'd be funny to put a wedge between us or maybe he had a bet with Brandon, who conveniently pushed me toward him, on screwing with me.

As I take my seat at the desk in the corner of the room, I admit to myself that I highly doubt either scenario is true—or if it was at the beginning, it's not now.

At least I hope.

Being with Dylan, or *talking* and kissing or whatever we're doing in this annoying undefined gray area, is like having the tip of a knife in my gut. I don't know if he's going to slice me open or just hold it there to spur me forward into action.

A tiny part of my brain wonders if James was right all along.

Innocent.

Cute.

Predictable.

I shake that off. It's not who I am anymore. Or maybe it is, but there are other things that take precedence over that.

I'm pulled out of my musings when James and Dylan

both enter the room, followed closely by one of the office administrators.

They both pointedly avoid me, but I see the forced blank expression on Dylan's face just as clearly as I see the purple and black bruise coming along nicely on James's.

"This is in-school suspension, not social hour," the administrator says. "You will only leave this room to use the bathroom or come directly to me with questions. Myself and teachers will check in periodically to ensure you are all on task and working on schoolwork. No phones or noise allowed."

The three of us are silent during her monologue. I'm mentally willing her to leave so I can get my thoughts together and figure out how to best confront Dylan. It's a horrible idea to do it in front of James, but I'm not sure I can hold it in all day.

"Am I understood?" she asks.

"Yes." I'm the only one who answers, but it's suitable enough for her to leave us alone and shut the door behind her.

I expect James and Dylan to pick up where they left off on Friday, but they both seem content pretending as if no one else is in the room.

To my surprise, they both appear to be working.

On schoolwork.

And I'm not.

I have no motivation with everything swirling in my head. I dig through my bag for something to distract me, but all I come up with is a few candy wrappers and my copy of *Brave New World* that makes me shake with emotion until I shove it back into the bottom.

I put my elbows on the table and my chin in my palms, and I'm content to stare at the wall.

My brain is receptive to the blank space, like I'm giving it room to breathe. I need things to be less chaotic so that I can decipher what's happening in my own head. It's a direct result of what these two boys, who I'm stuck here with, have put me through.

For most of the day, we're left alone. Occasionally, a teacher will pop in to briefly see that there are no more black eyes being doled out, but it's always during a break between classes.

During the period that should be English, I turn on my chair and watch Dylan work. It seems appropriate, given that we've shared this time together for months.

I'm trying to see what he's working on, what has him so enthralled during this exceptionally long day, but he's holding his textbook at an angle I can't see from where I'm sitting.

I scoot my chair forward, and without even looking up, he tilts the book a fraction, ensuring I can't see what he's up to.

Finally, I break.

"Is that today's assignment?" I ask him.

My voice is too loud, or it just seems that way because it has been too long since any of us has spoken.

Dylan doesn't bother answering me, but James turns to watch me attempt to break through this invisible wall that Dylan has put up around himself.

"I asked you if that was today's assignment," I say quieter this time, but my words are still sharp.

He's concentrating on ignoring me. I've stared at his

side profile enough times to know when he's reading and when he's avoiding, and he's definitely doing the latter right now, which only further infuriates me.

I wish I could gut him with a neutral, bored tone like he has mastered, but I'm angry and not as emotionally stunted into hiding myself like he is.

"Or is that one of your makeup assignments that you got permission from Miss Delway to do?" I say the words through gritted teeth. "That you so desperately needed my help to fulfill?"

He stops focusing on the words in front of him as I speak.

"The ones that she seemed to have no recollection of this morning, funny enough. Absolutely no idea what I was talking about. Imagine that."

He grips his pen and sucks in his bottom lip, trying to figure out the best way to talk his way out of this. I won't let him.

"Tell me why you lied," I demand.

He finally looks over at me, but he tilts his head toward James to remind me that we're not alone.

"I want the truth," I say evenly. "And I don't care if James is here and has to hear this. I certainly don't give a crap about your petty schoolyard rivalry and how mad you still are that he stood up to your bullying—"

"*My* bullying?" Dylan says incredulously. "That's a joke, right?"

"What part of this is funny?" I ask.

Dylan's gaze flickers up to the ceiling as if he's calling up to someone in the sky for reinforcements. "Your perception is so skewed."

I hate how he turned this conversation away from me getting answers on him lying to me, but I'm curious enough to hear him out. Dylan doesn't do anything unintentionally.

In fact, if these past few months have proved anything, it's that I should hear him out. "What makes you say that?"

"Tell me what you remember about that day," Dylan suggests. "Recess, fourth grade, the punch."

"Are you insinuating I'm an unreliable narrator in my own head?"

Dylan levels with me. "Don't you want to write *fiction*? Just humor me."

I run a frustrated hand through my curls, and my fingers graze the little rebellious lotus flowers when I do.

"I remember you and James arguing," I recall, picturing the now somewhat fuzzy scene in my mind. "I watched it happen from my spot across the playground until it looked like you two were about to start fighting. I walked over and caught the tail end of you insulting him, saying something about him being an idiot and then when you started to turn it around on me—"

"You punched me," Dylan says sourly. "That part is accurate."

"And the rest isn't?"

James watches us banter with a hard expression on his face. He refuses to meet my eyes, causing a pit to form in my stomach.

"James?" I say hesitantly.

Dylan sighs. "James and his little gang of tough guys wouldn't leave me alone because I didn't want to play with them. Apparently it was a slight that I'd rather sit by

241

myself instead of getting filthy with them. When I attempted to ask him why it was perfectly acceptable for his best friend to be a lonely bookworm and not me—"

"I thought you were making fun of me," I say, piecing it together.

It's not often in life you can pinpoint a moment that caused a domino effect of decisions, but this is one of them.

Without hesitation, I took James's side. That one instance colored my perception of Dylan for the years to come, viewing him as nothing but an entitled jerk who hated us because we weren't good enough by his standards.

I wish I could go back and rethink every single thing James told me about Dylan, but I can't even begin to think about how wrong I was.

"I'm so sorry, Dylan," I tell him, purposely using his first name to reach him on some sort of deep emotional level.

Whatever response he expected me to have, it was not an apology.

A rare flicker of surprise crosses his face, and he doesn't know what to do with it other than suppress it and fix his mask of indifference on it once again.

"Oh, come on, H, you're letting him play with your emotions," James says. "A sob story from elementary school and suddenly you feel bad for him?"

I can't even begin to unpack all of my baggage with James right now, so I keep my focus on Dylan.

"But it doesn't make sense...why did you lie to me?" I ask him. "You don't need my help. Was it, I don't know, a game or something? Coming full circle somehow?"

He works his jaw. "It's not like that," he insists, and I believe him.

Given what I know about his family and upbringing, he views self-preservation as a necessity.

I'm slowly realizing that he made up this entire ruse to spend time with me. I don't know why, exactly, but I have a hunch, and it's not one I want explained to me right now during in-school suspension.

He opens his mouth to speak, to be vulnerable to me in front of someone who he deeply hates, but as annoyed as I am, I'm not cruel.

Now is not the time for his grand gesture—and I'm not even sure I want one of those; I just want him to make it right between us.

"It's fine," I say before he can begin.

The look of relief is instant.

"You're kidding me, right?" James groans.

I turn to him, and although my insides are boiling, I'm calm on the surface. "James, I've spent the last six years supporting you at every single one of your track events, which are ridiculously boring about ninety percent of the time. I've consoled you after your relationships ended. I've listened to you complain about Dylan. I've been the best friend I could be. And you know what? You haven't been."

"You're mad so you're just going to take it out on me by leaving me high and dry at Cornell? And having me find this out from *him*?"

"You've just assumed I'll follow you around, supporting you and defending you and will just constantly *be there for you*, but you know what? I'm not doing it anymore."

"Finally," Dylan says under his breath.

JENNIFER ANN SHORE

"You're not involved with this," James nearly shouts. "Keep your little comments to yourself."

Dylan laughs. "Not involved? If it weren't for me, she'd still be trailing you around like a little puppy on a leash."

"Will both of you just shut the hell up?" I snap.

That stuns them both into angry, tense silence.

I spend the rest of the day willing the minutes to go by faster.

20

James spends the last week of school leading up to prom and graduation profusely apologizing.

He leaves notes in my locker, comes over every night, and spends our entire lunch hour trying to pull me back in.

I finally relent and accept his apology during Independent Study just so that he will leave me alone.

Dylan, on the other hand, completely ignores me. It doesn't help that in almost every instance we're in proximity, James is there, trailing along.

But still, I took a leap in him; in helping him and forgiving him, but I can't be in any sort of one-sided relationship with anyone anymore. Not my best friend, not someone I'm *talking* to, not anyone who comes along in the future.

Part of me wants to just purge every memory of both of them from my brain. I know I need space; I've been stuck in a suffocating whirlwind of their rivalry for so many years and I need some time to get distance and recalibrate my brain.

Unfortunately, as my mother and sister both remind me, I need to put that aside for now. In their minds, prom is one of those once-in-a-lifetime experiences.

"You'll have plenty of time over the summer to crawl into a hole of introspection," Audrey says to me over the phone. "But for now, accept James's offer and go for it. You guys will work through your garbage, but please, I'm asking you, as your only and favorite sister, to put everything else aside and enjoy a high school rite of passage. And I *need* to see you in that dress."

When my mom and I found the dress, I imagined being a different person while wearing it, like I would have a true Cinderella moment and it would be a magical night to remember forever, but I'm disappointed.

As I stand in the foyer and scrutinize my appearance, I'm already starting to regret this decision.

My hair is as wild and curly as it always is, but my mom used half a bottle of her fancy smoothing serum to defrizz it for me. My make-up is minimal, but I have a red lip, matching the exact shade of the dress.

From the front, it's a conservative look. It's a floor-length gown that's fitted and soft. It's sleeveless, but the neck is high and ties around. The tendrils from the bow hang down, tickling my bare skin that's exposed completely from shoulder to my lower back.

If James hadn't asked me, I wonder if Dylan would have. We've definitely gotten more comfortable around each other in public, and if the fight on the track had ended in a different way, I bet the entire school would be talking about him and me walking away hand in hand instead of the epic non-fight between him and James.

When I showed up on Dylan's doorstep in Audrey's borrowed clothes and preferred style, he told me that clothes are supposed to make you feel like a more confident version of yourself. Would he think that about this? Or would he think I'm a fraud?

This dress says a woman is practical, bold, and maybe wants to be a little devilish.

Not cute.

Not innocent.

Not predictable.

I put a smile on my face when James and his parents arrive. They force us to take an insufferable number of pictures together. One of us in front of the fireplace. Another one in the yard. While I put on his boutonniere. As he slides the corsage on my wrist.

There are jokes made by his parents—that I do not laugh at—about how it'll be nice for our children to see these one day.

My mom picks up on my discomfort and makes a point to tell me that I look stunning, and I ignore the tears in her and my dad's eyes when we drive off.

Out of habit, James reaches for my hand across the arm rest while he drives, but I don't take it.

"Sorry," he mumbles. "For what it's worth, though, you do look beautiful, H."

"Thank you," I say, turning to appraise how sleek he looks in his tuxedo. "You do, too."

"I believe you're supposed to tell me I look 'handsome.'"

"Gender norms are so exhausting," I tell him. "Plus, I'm the wannabe writer here. I get to choose the words I use."

He smiles. "Speaking of exhausting, have our parents always been like that?"

"Which part? Forcing us to pose and smile like we're dolls or pushing us toward the altar?"

"Both," he says with a laugh. "I guess I just was blind to it before."

It's pleasant to have a mutual feeling with him over this, and it gives me hope for being on the right track to mending our friendship. At that thought, I do reach out and squeeze his hand briefly before returning it to my own lap.

"James, we're going to be fine," I reassure him.

"I know," he says. "And for what it's worth, I *am* sorry for not treating you like I should have."

I guess I'm not the only one who has been doing some deep soul searching and evaluating lately.

"I don't think I can take any more apologies from you," I admit. "I'm a little burned out for a while."

"Well, I feel like I still need to make up for some stuff." He tries, and fails, to smooth his hair down. "You know, you've never really yelled at me like that before."

"Get used to it," I say immediately.

We both break out in grins, and the night moves along much more smoothly after that.

Our groove isn't as comfortable as it once was, but I don't think that's a bad thing.

Prom technically includes dinner, dancing, and an area for card games for those who aren't interested in dancing. I think most people are just biding their time until they can head to one of the afterparties in the hotel rooms above the grand ballroom.

The night feels like I imagined it would. The lights are dim and romantic. The dresses are gorgeous, and the suits are sleek. It's a big event that's already going to be a source of nostalgia when I'm older.

I try to enjoy it.

James insists on dancing to a few fast songs, which is something I've never been entirely comfortable with. We smile through it, though, and he spins me into some sort of swing dancing formation that makes my sides hurt with laughter.

When the music turns slow, he holds out his hand in silent request. I accept it, and he pulls me close. I don't recognize the song, but it's nice to sway to while James holds firm on my waist.

My head falls to his chest, and I close my eyes, breathing in him and this moment together.

I love James like he's family. He's home to me. We've spent so much time together, living and growing, but we're both getting to the point where we're ready to expand our perspectives.

While it would have been nice to have someone I know to be with me through this next stage of life, exploring my dream city and trying to find myself in it, I'm glad to know that James is going to be doing the same thing for himself.

I'm embarrassed that it took me this long to get to this point.

I've always considered myself fiercely independent and in charge of my own life, but it didn't click until Dylan forced his personality into my daily life for me to realize just how much I still had to work on with myself.

And that's the point of being with someone, isn't it?

Not just *talking* but actually challenging the person's viewpoint and helping them better themselves while enjoying every second along the way?

Well, maybe not every single second—Dylan can act like a stuck-up diva sometimes.

But even if we only have the summer together, I want to spend it exploring the long, warm days with him and his high-class standards that are infuriating and hilarious to me.

I jerk away from James before the song ends.

"I've been wondering when you were going to do that," he admits. "I'm impressed you lasted this long."

"I feel bad leaving you, but…"

He kisses my forehead. "I know."

I pull him in for a final fierce hug, and when we break, he pulls out his car keys and offers them to me.

It's a big deal.

James is so particular about his car, and if this is his final gesture of apology, I'm going to accept it whole-heartedly.

"Just tell me you won't wreck it."

"I won't."

"And that I won't lose you, H. That you'll still be my best friend?"

"Always," I promise, accepting the keys from his outstretched hand.

I speed to Dylan's house with the windows down and the music up.

I'm back again, on his doorstep, but I don't bother texting him because I know—or at least I hope—that he's home alone.

Brandon, Kyle, and almost every other recognizable face are still in the ballroom, and since his father is on the board of the school, both he and Mrs. Archer are there, too, mingling with the other parents and waiting for the event to officially be over.

I ring the doorbell multiple times until Dylan appears.

"Hi," I say when he opens the door.

His eyes rake over my dress in approval. "Reed, you're looking better than the last time you showed up on my doorstep unannounced."

I smooth down my hair. "I have something I wanted to say."

He leans against the doorframe, and I'm conscious of just how much I want to fall into his chest.

I swallow. "I don't know why you lied about needing my help, but to be honest, I don't really care. Because whatever your intentions were in the beginning, I think that the result of whatever this is between us overpowers anything else."

Dylan doesn't move a muscle, so I continue.

"I may not fit into your life, with the yacht club and the table manners. I think I'm too messy and bookish and boring for what you're used to, but I'm real, Dylan. I'm the real deal, and when I tell you that I love you, that I'm in love with you, and it's so stupid because we're so young and it's all happened so fast, but it's the truth."

"You think you love me?" Dylan says with a strained voice.

I shake my head. "I know it."

Dylan steps aside, granting me permission into his grand foyer.

It's no less impressive now than it was the first time I stepped in it, so I give myself a moment to take it all in while I try to stop my hands from shaking and wait to see what he's going to say back.

I told him I loved him, after all.

Surely that warrants some sort of response—at minimum, an apology I was hoping to hear from him all week.

I turn and catch him staring at my exposed back. "Dylan?" I say so quietly it's like a whisper.

He shuts the door and grabs my hand. It's not a rough hold, necessarily, but it's firm and full of purpose.

We're heading up toward his bedroom, which makes sense. Even if his parents aren't home yet, they eventually will be, and he probably wants privacy for what he has to say. But we pass his room, or at least which door I think it is, and we wind to the very end of the hallway on the second floor.

He pauses outside the door, taking a big breath in before he turns the knob.

When he flicks the light switch, I gasp.

The massive room has high, vaulted ceilings with floor to ceiling windows, but that's not what catches me.

Painted canvases, all in varying degrees of completion, are everywhere. They're stacked up in the rafters, hanging on the walls, and leaning against one of the glass windows.

I'm awed, but given the fact that Mrs. Archer owns an art gallery, I'm not totally surprised she has such an incredible collection of work here. I wonder if artists come by and work here or something.

Dylan watches me take in the room with heavy expectation in his eyes.

It startles me, as if I'm missing a piece to the puzzle, until I nearly step on a giant canvas that's taking up a third of the floor.

"Oh," I say as my eyes are reflected into my own painted ones.

The painting isn't totally finished, but I recognize myself in it instantly—the wild hair, the eyes, and Audrey's borrowed lotus earrings.

I'm depicted in black, white, and gray, but I kind of blur out at my neck, fading into the background. The only thing that's shown and contrasted on the lower half of the painting is a beautifully crafted heart with all shades of red.

Instantly I'm reminded of the Yarra DeLinch painting that hangs in Mrs. Archer's gallery, and the connecting dots stun me.

"What's your middle name?" I ask quietly.

"Isaac."

He steps toward me with his hands loose at his side.

Yarra DeLinch

Dylan I. Archer

The letters rearrange in my head.

"Anagram," I say, and it's the only word I can form.

He nods and steps toward me, seeing up close how I'm digesting this information.

His expression is hard and protective, but if there's anything I've learned about what I've just seen, how he views me, it's that he's just as shattered as the rest of us inside.

Humans are full of complexities, and most of them don't ever get vocalized. There's something almost too fragile about admitting the deepest parts of yourself aloud, and both Dylan and I struggle with it in that regard.

We can't say it aloud, but we can say it with ink.

For me, it's words on a page, written or typed.

For him, it's art on canvas.

This beautiful painting is the way he is showing me how he feels.

It's an incredible gesture, but I just stood on his front porch and vocalized my feelings, told him that I loved him, out loud with my own voice, and I need him to do the same.

"What are you trying to tell me?" I ask, gesturing to the work and the vacant space between him and me.

He shoves his hands in his pockets and looks at the piece as he speaks.

"I didn't know how to connect with you. I mean, what was I supposed to do? Tell you that even though you hate me, I've been watching you since we were kids, and I felt a certain connection to you that you did not reciprocate in any way, shape, or form? That even though we're both lonely and neurotic, we didn't have to be so alone? That I've spent just as much time being frustrated by your tenacity as I've loved every single thought and word that has come from your mouth? That I've dreamed of what it would be like to claim you and those curls for my own selfish interest?"

Dylan, once again, turns to me. "I panicked. I realized I

was missing my chance with you, Harper. That we had such little time left of school, and I had wasted the years, letting Lawson's hatred of me ruin everything. I came up with the stupid cover story that I needed help because I thought it was the only way I could approach you, and honestly, it worked, didn't it? We got to know each other, the real versions of ourselves, even though it was based on a lie."

My hands are shaking, but I reach out for him, silently begging him to come closer.

When he pulls me into his arms, I trace the little meteor scar below his eye. "Was it all worth it?" I ask.

"Redoing assignments and arguing about them isn't my favorite type of foreplay, but it'll do," he says.

I kiss the classic Dylan Archer smirk right off his face.

EPILOGUE

Given how ridiculous everyone looks in a cap and gown, I can't say I appreciate the historical significance or need to continue the tradition—but I do count it as a win that I got the school board to scrap the valedictorian speech and the alphabetization of the procession.

We've all spent so much time over the years in uniforms that it just feels like one final way to trap us before we can unzip the gigantic cloaks and reveal our true natures and personal styles.

Not that I really have one, but it's the principle of it.

The dean of the school has been talking for the past forty minutes, and I don't think anyone is paying attention to whatever he is saying.

From my vantage point on the stage, where I'm seated with honor as the valedictorian, I see a number of people, mostly grandparents and younger siblings, nodding off in the bleachers.

In the crowd of graduating seniors, most of them are

flipping through the yearbooks that they collected in the morning and having others sign them.

Once the procession begins, I get to shake hands with each of my classmates before they're greeted by other school officials. Then the dean hands them their diplomas and announces which college they'll be attending.

Most students are going to an Ivy League school, but a handful are attending local colleges, joining the military, or going straight into the workforce.

It's kind of boring, but I'm just glad I don't have to make a speech.

James makes me laugh as I shake his hand and then he greets the others on the stage before he's handed his diploma.

"James Lawson," the dean says. "Is heading to…"

"Cornell," James says proudly.

Although it's picked up by the microphone, the dean repeats it for the crowd, and there are a number of claps and cheers for him.

A few other people from the track team follow behind James, and then Brandon, who I know is going to the University of Pittsburgh while he splits his time with his charity work, is announced.

Dylan is the last one on the team to step up to the stage, and he drops a kiss on my cheek while he shakes my hand.

I bite my lip to stop the gigantic grin that wants to take over my face as I wait for the announcement of his name and school.

He acknowledges his father at the end of the stage, who

is standing with all the other school board members, and all he gets is a curt head nod in return.

Despite everything Dylan and I have been through, he's been exceptionally coy about his plans after the summer, and I have given up on pushing the issue.

I'm more eager than anyone in the audience for the answer to the dean's prompt.

Dylan gets a warm greeting from the dean. "Dylan Archer is going to...let me guess, Harvard? Dartmouth?"

Dylan glances at his father, who is stone faced, and then me before he says, "Pratt Institute."

"Pratt Institute?" There's a ripple of surprise that makes it through the group of students and a few parents in the stands. "I don't believe I've heard of it before."

Dylan brushes off his remarks and holds his hand out, waiting for his diploma. The dean remembers himself and awards it to him, then prepares to receive the next student.

Instead of the normal claps and cheers, the crowd murmurs.

Being an Archer comes with many expectations, and the ones they had for him just shattered.

If we were still in school, it would be all everyone could talk about for the next week, gossiping about how they can't believe he's going to some private art school in Brooklyn when he could be rubbing elbows with future politicians and business game changers at a big school.

But thankfully, I'm completely oblivious to the drama now that I've collected my diploma and bid goodbye to a few of my classmates.

It's funny to me how people make high school problems seem like an entire world, but the moment we throw our caps into the air, it's all gone. The trivial worries about assignments and accidentally getting the same bag as someone else ceases to exist.

At least for now.

I've vowed to take the same advice Audrey gave me at the beginning of my senior year, only this time, I'm actually going to listen to it.

I'm going to enjoy what it means to be eighteen, and it's the only thing I'm thinking about as James and I are presented with the lighted candles on our birthday cake a few weeks after graduation.

Dylan's arms are around my waist. The feeling is blissful, but it's not exactly easy to be with him. We bicker and challenge each other. Dylan can be an entitled jerk, and I can be a hard-headed know-it-all.

He's constantly at odds with James, but they've managed to find a middle ground for this one night of our joint birthday party after we spent all day napping, swimming, and enjoying the sunshine on a rented boat with our families.

As the candles flicker and the birthday song ends, I look at Dylan and find that in this moment, I'm perfectly content.

I don't need to get lost in planning every single possibility of my future, of *our* potential future. I have nothing to wish for or plot out because I'm excited to live in the present.

Dylan squeezes my waist as my parents and Audrey smile at the two of us, then James and I blow the candles out together.

ACKNOWLEDGMENTS

I have to give some serious love to all of the bloggers out there who have supported me since the beginning—especially The Uncorked Librarian, N. N. Light, Tasty Itinerary, Sisters With A Booktique, and JM Bibliolater. You are all angels.

My editor, Taylor Starek, thank you for your patient needling with edits and suggestions—you help give my writing that much-needed nudge forward.

Kelly Lipovich, who designed another absolutely gorgeous cover, I am so grateful to have witnessed your brilliance in so many different settings over the years.

Lindsay Hallowell saves me from myself on a regular basis (because my heart loves typos but my head listens to you). Thank you for all the laughs and killing off my comma splices.

Rachel Kilroy, for being the best friend and book photographer I could have ever hoped for in this life. I love you so damn much.

To my friends and family, thank you for your encouragement, love, and excitement—I'm ridiculously lucky to have all you wonderful people in my corner.

ABOUT THE AUTHOR

Jennifer Ann Shore is a writer and an Amazon bestselling author based in Seattle, Washington.

She has written multiple fiction novels, including "New Wave," a young adult dystopian, and "The Extended Summer of Anna and Jeremy," a young adult romance.

In her decade of working in journalism, marketing, and book publishing, she has won numerous awards for her work from companies such as Hearst and SIIA.

Be sure to visit her website (https://www. jenniferannshore.com) and follow her on Twitter (@JenniferAShore), Instagram (@shorely), or your preferred social media channel to stay in touch.